The Meaning of Liff

"This is the kind of book one feels one might be
invited to own by American Express"
J. B. Preestley

Douglas Adams and
John Lloyd

The Meaning
of Liff

Pan Books
and Faber & Faber

First published simultaneously 1983
by Pan Books Ltd.
Cavaye Place, London SW10 9PG
and Faber & Faber Limited
19 18 17
© Douglas Adams and John Lloyd 1983
ISBN 0 330 28121 6
Photoset by Parker Typesetting Service, Leicester
Printed and bound in Great Britain by
Cox & Wyman Ltd, Reading

With grateful thanks to Jane Belson, Gaye
Green, Sean Hardie, Alex Catto, Helen Rhys Jones.
Laurie Rowley, Peter Spence and Caroline Warner for
some of the more interesting and repellent
ideas in this book.

In Life*, there are many hundreds of common experiences, feelings, situations and even objects which we all know and recognize, but for which no words exist.

On the other hand, the world is littered with thousands of spare words which spend their time doing nothing but loafing about on signposts pointing at places.

Our job, as we see it, is to get these words down off the signposts and into the mouths of babes and sucklings and so on, where they can start earning their keep in everyday conversation and make a more positive contribution to society.

Douglas Adams
John Lloyd

*And, indeed, in Liff.

N

Aith

Aird
of Sleat

Ardslignish

Aboyne
Aldclune

Ardscalpsie

Articlave

Aasleagh

Ardscull   Agglethorpe   Ainderby Steeple
                                 Ainderby Quernhow
Ardcrony
                  Amwlch   Ainsworth
Araglin   Ahenny   Aigburth
                            Alltami
Adrigole
                  Aberystwyth

                  Abercrave   Acle
                  Aberbeeg
                        Aynho
                       Adlestrop
                                    Amersham
              Affpuddle   Abinger

Aasleagh (n.)
A liqueur made only for drinking at the end of a revoltingly long bottle party when all the drinkable drink has been drunk.

Aberbeeg (vb.)
Of amateur actors, to adopt a Mexican accent when called upon to play any variety of foreigner (except Pakistanis – for whom a Welsh accent is considered sufficient).

Abercrave (vb.)
To strongly desire to swing from the pole on the rear footplate of a bus.

Aberystwyth (n.)
A nostalgic yearning which is in itself more pleasant than the thing being yearned for.

Abilene (adj.)
Descriptive of the pleasing coolness on the reverse side of the pillow.

ABINGER (n.)
One who washes up everything except the frying pan, the cheese grater and the saucepan which the chocolate sauce has been made in.

ABOYNE (vb.)
To beat an expert at a game of skill by playing so appallingly that none of his clever tactics or strategies are of any use to him.

ACLE (n.)
The rogue pin which shirtmakers conceal in the most improbable fold of a new shirt. Its function is to stab you when you don the garment.

ADLESTROP (n.)
That part of a suitcase which is designed to get snarled up on conveyor belts at airports. Some of the more modern adlestrop designs have a special 'quick release' feature which enables the case to flip open at this point and fling your underclothes into the conveyor belt's gearing mechanism.

ADRIGOLE (n.)
The centrepiece of a merry-go-round on which the man with the tickets stands unnervingly still.

AFFCOT (n.)
The sort of fart you hope people will talk after.

AFFPUDDLE (n.)
A puddle which is hidden under a pivoted paving stone. You only know it's there when you step on the paving stone and the puddle shoots up your leg.

AGGLETHORPE (n.)
A dispute between two pooves in a boutique.

AHENNY (adj.)
The way people stand when examining other people's bookshelves.

AIGBURTH (n.)
Any piece of readily identifiable anatomy found amongst cooked meat.

AINDERBY QUERNHOW (n.)
One who continually bemoans the 'loss' of the word 'gay' to the English language, even though they had never used the word in any context at all until they started complaining that they couldn't use it any more.

AINDERBY STEEPLE (n.)
One who asks you a question with the apparent motive of wanting to hear your answer, but who cuts short your opening sentence by leaning forward and saying 'and I'll tell you why I ask . . .' and then talking solidly for the next hour.

AINSWORTH (n.)
The length of time it takes to get served in a camera shop. Hence, also, how long we will have to wait for the abolition of income tax or the Second Coming.

AIRD OF SLEAT (n. archaic)
Ancient Scottish curse placed from afar on the stretch of land now occupied by Heathrow Airport.

AITH (n.)
The single bristle that sticks out sideways on a cheap paintbrush.

Albuquerque (n.)
A shapeless squiggle which is utterly unlike your normal signature, but which is, nevertheless, all you are able to produce when asked formally to identify yourself.

Muslims, whose religion forbids the making of graven images, use albuquerques to decorate their towels, menu cards and pyjamas.

Aldclune (n.)
One who collects ten-year-old telephone directories.

Alltami (n.)
The ancient art of being able to balance the hot and cold shower taps.

Ambleside (n.)
A talk given about the Facts of Life by a father to his son whilst walking in the garden on a Sunday afternoon.

Amersham (n.)
The sneeze which tickles but never comes.

(Thought to derive from the Metropolitan Line tube station of the same name where the rails always rattle but the train never arrives.)

Amlwch (n.)
A British Rail sandwich which has been kept soft by being regularly washed and resealed in clingfilm.

Araglin (n. archaic)
A medieval practical joke played by young squires on a knight aspirant the afternoon he is due to start his vigil. As the knight arrives at the castle the squires attempt to raise the drawbridge very suddenly as the knight and his charger step on to it.

Ardcrony (n.)
A remote acquaintance passed off as 'a very good friend of mine' by someone trying to impress people.

Ardscalpsie (n.)
Excuse made by rural Welsh hairdresser for completely massacring your hair.

Ardscull (n.)
Excuse made by rural Welsh hairdresser for deep wounds inflicted on your scalp in an attempt to rectify whatever it was that induced the ardscalpsie (q.v.)

Ardslignish (adj.)
Adjective which describes the behaviour of Sellotape when you are tired.

Articlave (n.)
A clever architectural construction designed to give the illusion from the top deck of a bus that it is far too big for the road.

Aynho (vb.)
Of waiters, never to have a pen.

B

BABWORTH (n.)
Something which justifies having a really good cry.

BALDOCK (n.)
The sharp prong on the top of a tree stump where the tree has snapped off before being completely sawn through.

BALLYCUMBER (n.)
One of the six half-read books lying somewhere in your bed.

BANFF (adj.)
Pertaining to, or descriptive of, that kind of facial expression which is impossible to achieve except when having a passport photograph taken.

BANTEER (n. archaic)
A lusty and raucous old ballad sung after a particularly spectacular araglin (q.v.) has been pulled off.

Barstibley (n.)
A humorous device such as a china horse or small naked porcelain infant which jocular hosts use to piss water into your Scotch with.

Baughurst (n.)
That kind of large fierce ugly woman who owns a small fierce ugly dog.

Baumber (n.)
A fitted elasticated bottom sheet which turns your mattress banana-shaped.

Bealings (pl. n. archaic)
The unsavoury parts of a moat which a knight has to pour out of his armour after being the victim of an araglin (q.v.).

In medieval Flanders, soup made from bealings was a very slightly sought-after delicacy.

Beaulieu Hill (n.)
The optimum vantage point from which one to view people undressing in the bedroom across the street.

Beccles (pl. n.)
The small bone buttons placed in bacon sandwiches by unemployed guerrilla dentists.

Bedfont (n.)
A lurching sensation in the pit of the stomach experienced at breakfast in a hotel, occasioned by the realisation that it is about now that the chambermaid will have discovered the embarrassing stain on your bottom sheet.

Belper (n.)
A knob of someone else's chewing gum which you unexpectedly find your hand resting on under a desk top, under the passenger seat of your car or on somebody's thigh under their skirt.

Benburb (n.)
The sort of man who becomes a returning officer.

Berepper (n.)
The irrevocable and sturdy fart released in the presence of royalty, which sounds quite like a small motorbike passing by (but not enough to be confused with one).

BERKHAMSTED (n.)
The massive three-course midmorning blow-out enjoyed by a dieter who has already done his or her slimming duty by having a teaspoonful of cottage cheese for breakfast.

BERRY POMEROY (n.)
1. The shape of a gourmet's lips.
2. The droplet of saliva which hangs from them.

BILBSTER (n.)
A pimple so hideous and enormous that you have to cover it with sticking plaster and pretend you've cut yourself shaving.

BISHOP'S CAUNDLE (n.)
An opening gambit before a game of chess whereby the missing pieces are replaced by small ornaments from the mantelpiece.

BLEAN (n.)
Scientific measure of luminosity:
   1 glimmer = 100,000 bleans.
   Usherettes' torches are designed to produce between 2.5 and 4 bleans, enabling them to assist you in falling downstairs, treading on people or

putting your hand into a Neapolitan tub when reaching for change.

Blithbury (n.)
A look someone gives you by which you become aware that they're much too drunk to have understood anything you've said to them in the last twenty minutes.

Blitterlees (pl. n.)
The little slivers of bamboo picked off a cane chair by a nervous guest which litter the carpet beneath and tell the chair's owner that the whole piece of furniture is about to uncoil terribly and slowly until it resembles a giant pencil sharpening.

Bodmin (n.)
The irrational and inevitable discrepancy between the amount pooled and the amount needed when a large group of people try to pay a bill together after a meal.

Bolsover (n.)
One of those brown plastic trays with bumps on, placed upside down in boxes of chocolates to make you think you're getting two layers.

BONKLE (n.)
Of plumbing in old hotels, to make loud and unexplained noises in the night, particularly at about five o'clock in the morning.

BOOLTEENS (pl. n.)
The small scatterings of foreign coins and half-p's which inhabit dressing tables. Since they are never used and never thrown away boolteens account for a significant drain on the world's money supply.

BOOTHBY GRAFFOE (n.)
1. The man in the pub who slaps people on the back as if they were old friends, when in fact he has no friends, largely on account of this habit.
2. Any story told by Robert Morley on chat shows.

BOSCASTLE (n.)
A huge pyramid of tin cans placed just inside the entrance to a supermarket.

BOSEMAN (n.)
One who spends all day loafing about near pedestrian crossings looking as if he's about to cross.

BOTCHERBY (n.)
The principle by which British roads are signposted.

BOTLEY (n.)
The prominent stain on a man's trouser crotch seen on his return from the lavatory. A botley proper is caused by an accident with the push taps, and should not be confused with any stain caused by insufficient waggling of the willy (see: piddletrenthide).

BOTOLPHS (n.)
Huge benign tumours which arch-deacons and old chemistry teachers affect to wear on the sides of their noses.

BOTUSFLEMING (n. medical)
A small, long-handled steel trowel used by surgeons to remove the contents of a patient's nostrils prior to a sinus operation.

BRADFORD (n.)
A school teacher's old hairy jacket, now severely discoloured by chalk dust, ink, egg and the precipitations of unedifying chemical reactions.

BRADWORTHY (n.)
One who is skilled in the art of naming loaves.

BRECON (n. anatomical term)
That part of the toenail which is designed to snag on nylon sheets.

BRISBANE (n.)
A perfectly reasonable explanation. (Such as the one offered by a person with a gurgling cough which has nothing to do with the fact that they smoke fifty cigarettes a day.)

BROATS (pl. n.)
A pair of trousers with a career behind them. Broats are most commonly seen on elderly retired army officers. Originally the broats were part of their best suit back in the thirties; then in the fifties they were demoted and used for gardening. Recently, pensions not being what they were, the broats have been called out of retirement and reinstated as part of the best suit again.

BROMPTON (n.)
A brompton is that which is said to have been committed when you are convinced you are about to blow off

with a resounding trumpeting noise in a public place and all that actually slips out is a tiny 'pfpt'.

BROMSGROVE (n.)
Any urban environment containing a small amount of dogturd and about forty-five tons of bent steel pylon or a lump of concrete with holes claiming to be sculpture.

'Oh, come my dear, and come with me

And wander 'neath the bromsgrove tree' – Betjeman.

BROUGH SOWERBY (n.)
One who has been working at the same desk in the same office for fifteen years and has very much his own ideas about why he is continually passed over for promotion.

BRUMBY (n.)
The fake antique plastic seal on a pretentious whisky bottle.

BRYMBO (n.)
The single unappetising bun left in a baker's shop after four p.m.

Budby (n)
A nipple clearly defined through flimsy or wet material.

Bude (n.)
A polite joke reserved for use in the presence of vicars.

Buldoo (n.)
A virulent red-coloured pus which generally accompanies clonmult (q.v.) and sadberge (q.v.).

Burbage (n.)
The sound made by a liftful of people all trying to breathe politely through their noses.

Bures (n. medical)
The scabs on knees and elbows formed by a compulsion to make love on cheap Habitat floor-matting.

Burleston (n., vb.)
That peculiarly tuneless humming and whistling adopted by people who are extremely angry.

Burlingjobb (n. archaic)
A seventeenth-century crime by which excrement is thrown into the street from a ground-floor window.

Burnt Yates (pl. n.)
Condition to which yates (q.v.) will suddenly pass without any apparent intervening period, after the spirit of the throckmorton (q.v.) has finally been summoned by incessant throcking (q.v.).

Bursledon (n.)
The bluebottle one is too tired to get up and swat, but not tired enough to sleep through.

Burton Coggles (pl. n.)
A bunch of keys found in a drawer whose purpose has long been forgotten, and which can therefore now be used only for dropping down people's backs as a cure for nose-bleeds.

Burwash (n.)
The pleasurable cool sloosh of puddle water over the toes of your gumboots.

C

CAARNDUNCAN (n.)
The high-pitched and insistent cry of the young male human urging one of its peer group to do something dangerous on a cliff-edge or piece of toxic waste ground.

CAIRNPAT (n.)
A large piece of dried dung found in mountainous terrain above the cowline which leads the experienced tracker to believe that hikers have recently passed.

CAMER (n.)
A mis-tossed caber.

CANNOCK CHASE (n.)

In any box of After Eight Mints, there is always a large number of empty envelopes and no more than four or five actual mints. The cannock chase is the process by which, no matter which part of the box you insert your fingers into, or how often, you will always extract most of the empty sachets before pinning down an actual mint, or 'cannock'.

The cannock chase also occurs with people who put their dead matches back in the matchbox, and then embarrass themselves at parties trying to light cigarettes with three quarters of an inch of charcoal.

The term is also used to describe futile attempts to pursue unscrupulous advertising agencies who nick your ideas to sell chocolates with.

CHENIES (pl. n.)

The last few sprigs or tassels of last Christmas's decorations you notice on the ceiling while lying on the sofa on an August afternoon.

CHICAGO (n.)

The foul-smelling wind which precedes an underground railway train.

CHIPPING ONGAR (n.)

The disgust and embarrassment (or 'ongar') felt by an observer in the presence of a person festooned with kirbies (q.v.), when they don't know them well enough to tell them to wipe them off. Invariably this 'ongar' is accompanied by an involuntary staccato twitching of the leg (or 'chipping').

CLABBY (adj.)

A 'clabby' conversation is one struck up by a commissionaire or cleaning lady in order to avoid any further actual work. The opening gambit is usually designed to provoke the maximum confusion, and therefore the longest possible clabby conversation. It is vitally important to learn the correct, or 'clixby' (q.v.), response to a clabby gambit, and not to get trapped by a 'ditherington' (q.v.). For instance, if confronted with a clabby gambit such as 'Oh, Mr Smith, I didn't know you'd had your leg off', the ditherington response is 'I haven't . . .' whereas the clixby is 'Good.'

CLACKAVOID (n.)

Technical BBC term for a page of dialogue from *Blake's Seven*.

CLACKMANNAN (n.)
The sound made by knocking over an elephant's-foot umbrella stand full of walking sticks.

Hence name for a particular kind of disco drum-riff.

CLATHY (adj.)
Nervously indecisive about how safely to dispose of a dud lightbulb.

CLENCHWARTON (n. archaic)
One who assists an exorcist by squeezing whichever part of the possessed the exorcist deems useful.

CLIXBY (adj.)
Politely rude. Briskly vague. Firmly uninformative.

CLONMULT (n.)
A yellow ooze usually found near secretions of buldoo (q.v.) and sadberge (q.v.).

CLOVIS (q.v.)
One who actually looks forward to putting up the Christmas decorations in the office.

CLUN (n.)
A leg which has gone to sleep and has to be hauled around after you.

CLUNES (pl. n.)
People who just won't go.

CONDOVER (n.)
One who is employed to stand about all day browsing through the magazine racks in the newsagent.

CONG (n.)
Strange-shaped metal utensil found at the back of the saucepan cupboard. Many authorities believe that congs provide conclusive proof of the existence of a now extinct form of yellow vegetable which the Victorians used to boil mercilessly.

Corfe (n.)
An object which is almost totally indistinguishable from a newspaper, the one crucial difference being that it belongs to somebody else and is unaccountably much more interesting than your own – which may otherwise appear to be in all respects identical.

Though it is a rule of life that a train or other public place may contain any number of corfes but only one newspaper, it is quite possible to transform your own perfectly ordinary newspaper into a corfe by the simple expedient of letting somebody else read it.

Corfu (n.)
The dullest person you met during the course of your holiday. Also the only one who failed to understand that the exchanging of addresses at the end of a holiday is merely a social ritual and is absolutely not an invitation to phone you up or turn up unannounced on your doorstep three months later.

Corriearklet (n.)
The moment at which two people, approaching from opposite ends of a long passageway, recognise each other and immediately pretend they

haven't. This is to avoid the ghastly embarrassment of having to *continue* recognising each other the whole length of the corridor.

CORRIECRAVIE (n.)
To avert the horrors of corrievorrie (q.v.) corriecravie is usually employed. This is the cowardly but highly skilled process by which both protagonists continue to approach while keeping up the pretence that they haven't noticed each other – by staring furiously at their feet, grimacing into a notebook, or studying the walls closely as if in a mood of deep irritation.

CORRIEDOO (n.)
The crucial moment of false recognition in a long passageway encounter. Though both people are perfectly well aware that the other is approaching, they must eventually pretend sudden recognition. They now look up with a glassy smile, as if having spotted each other for the first time, (and are *particularly* delighted to have done so) shouting out 'Haaaaalllllloooo!' as if to say 'Good grief!! You!! Here!! Of all people! Well I never. Coo. Stap me vitals, etc.'

CORRIEMOILLIE (n.)
The dreadful sinking sensation in a long passageway encounter when both protagonists immediately realise they have plumped for the corriedoo (q.v.) much too early as they are still a good thirty yards apart. They were embarrassed by the pretence of corriecravie (q.v .) and decided to make use of the corriedoo because they felt silly. This was a mistake as corrievorrie (q.v.) will make them seem far sillier.

CORRIEVORRIE (n.)
Corridor etiquette demands that once a corriedoo (q.v.) has been declared, corrievorrie must be employed. Both protagonists must now embellish their approach with an embarrassing combination of waving, grinning, making idiot faces, doing pirate impressions, and waggling the head from side to side while holding the other person's eyes as the smile drips off their face, until, with great relief, they pass each other.

CORRIEMUCHLOCH (n.)
Word describing the kind of person who can make a complete mess of a simple job like walking down a corridor.

CORSTORPHINE (n.)
A very short peremptory service held in monasteries prior to teatime to offer thanks for the benediction of digestive biscuits.

COTTERSTOCK (n.)
A piece of wood used to stir paint and thereafter stored uselessly in a shed in perpetuity.

CRAIL (n. mineral)
Crail is a common kind of rock or gravel found widely across the British Isles.

Each individual stone (due to an as yet undiscovered gravitational property) is charged with 'negative buoyancy'.

This means that no matter how much crail you remove from the garden, more of it will rise to the surface.

Crail is much employed by the Royal Navy for making the paperweights and ashtrays used inside submarines.

CRANLEIGH (n.)
A mood of irrational irritation with everyone and everything.

CROMARTY (n.)
The brittle sludge which clings to the top of ketchup bottles and plastic tomatoes in nasty cafés.

CURRY MALLET (n.)
A large wooden or rubber club which poachers use to despatch cats or other game which they can only sell to Indian restaurants. For particularly small cats the price obtainable is not worth the cost of expending ammunition.

Dalrymple (n.)
Dalrymples are the things you pay extra for on pieces of hand-made craftwork – the rough edges, the paint smudges and the holes in the glazing.

Damnaglaur (n.)
A certain facial expression which actors are required to demonstrate their mastery of before they are allowed to play Macbeth.

Darenth (n.)
Measure = 0.0000176 mg.
Defined as that amount of margarine capable of covering one hundred slices of bread to the depth of one molecule. This is the legal maximum allowed in sandwich bars in Greater London.

Deal (n.)
The gummy substance found between damp toes.

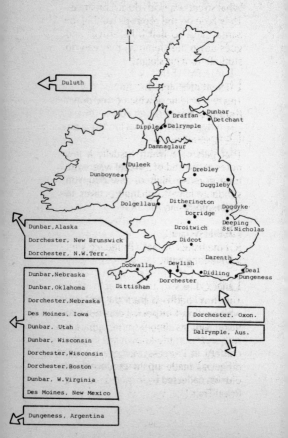

N

Duluth

Draffan
Dunbar
Dipple
Dalrymple
Detchant
Damnaglaur
Duleek
Drebley
Dunboyne
Duggleby
Dolgellau
Ditherington
Dogdyke
Dorridge
Deeping
Droitwich
St. Nicholas
Didcot
Darenth
Dobwalls
Dewlish
Deal
Dorchester
Didling
Dungeness
Dittisham

Dunbar, Alaska
Dorchester, New Brunswick
Dorchester, N.W.Terr.

Dunbar, Nebraska
Dunbar, Oklahoma
Dorchester, Nebraska
Des Moines, Iowa
Dunbar, Utah
Dunbar, Wisconsin
Dorchester, Wisconsin
Dorchester, Boston
Dunbar, W.Virginia
Des Moines, New Mexico

Dorchester, Oxon.

Dalrymple, Aus.

Dungeness, Argentina

DEEPING ST NICHOLAS (n.)
What street-wise kids do at Christmas. They hide on the rooftops waiting for Santa Claus so that if he arrives and goes down the chimney, they can rip stuff off from his sleigh.

DES MOINES (pl. n.)
The two little lines which come down from your nose.

DETCHANT (n.)
That part of a hymn (usually a few notes at the end of a verse) where the tune goes so high or low that you suddenly have to change octaves to accommodate it.

DEWLISH (adj.)
(Of the hands or feet.) Prunelike after an overlong bath.

DIDCOT (n.)
The tiny oddly-shaped bit of card which a ticket inspector cuts out of a ticket with his clipper for no apparent reason. It is a little-known fact that the confetti at Princess Margaret's wedding was made up of thousands of didcots collected by inspectors on the Royal Train.

DIDLING (participial vb.)
The process of trying to work out who did it when reading a whodunnit, and trying to keep your options open so that when you find out you can allow yourself to think that you knew perfectly well who it was all along.

DILLYTOP (n.)
The kind of bath plug which for some unaccountable reason is actually designed to sit on top of the hole rather than fit into it.

DIPPLE (vb.)
To try to remove a sticky something from one hand with the other, thus causing it to get stuck to the other hand and eventually to anything else you try to remove it with.

DITHERINGTON (n.)
Sudden access of panic experienced by one who realises that he is being drawn inexorably into a clabby (q.v.) conversation, i.e. one he has no hope of enjoying, benefiting from or understanding.

DITTISHAM (n.)
Any music you hear on the radio to which you have to listen very carefully to determine whether it is an advertising jingle or a bona fide record.

Dittishams are one of the two major reasons for the collapse of people's enthusiasm for rock. The other is Rod Stewart.

DOBWALLS (pl. n.)
The now hard-boiled bits of nastiness which have to be prised off crockery by hand after it has been through a dishwasher.

DOCKERY (n.)
Facetious behaviour adopted by an accused man in the mistaken belief that this will endear him to the judge.

DOGDYKE (vb.)
Of dog-owners, to adopt the absurd pretence that the animal shitting in the gutter is nothing to do with them.

DOLGELLAU (n.)
The clump, or cluster, of bored, quietly enraged, mildly embarrassed men waiting for their wives to come out of a changing room in a dress shop.

DORCHESTER (n.)
A throaty cough by someone else so timed as to obscure the crucial part of the rather amusing remark you've just made.

DORRIDGE (n.)
Technical term for one of the lame excuses written in very small print on the side of packets of food or washing powder to explain why there's hardly anything inside. Examples include 'Contents may have settled in transit' and 'To keep each biscuit fresh they have been individually wrapped in silver paper and cellophane and separated with corrugated lining, a cardboard flap, and heavy industrial tyres.'

DRAFFAN (n.)
An infuriating person who always manages to look much more dashing than anyone else by turning up unshaven and hungover at a formal party.

DREBLEY (n.)
Name for a shop which is supposed to be witty but is in fact wearisome, e.g. 'The Frock Exchange', 'Hair Apparent', etc.

Droitwich (n.)
A street dance. The two partners approach from opposite directions and try politely to get out of each other's way. They step to the left, step to the right, apologise, step to the left again, apologise again, bump into each other and repeat as often as unnecessary.

Dubuque (n.)
A look given by a superior person to someone who has arrived wearing the wrong sort of shoes.

Duddo (n.)
The most deformed potato in any given collection of potatoes.

Duggleby (n.)
The person in front of you in the supermarket queue who has just unloaded a bulging trolley on to the conveyor belt and is now in the process of trying to work out which pocket they left their cheque book in, and indeed which pair of trousers.

Duleek (n.)
Sudden realisation, as you lie in bed waiting for the alarm to go off, that it should have gone off an hour ago.

DULUTH (adj.)
The smell of a taxi out of which people have just got.

DUNBAR (n.)
A highly specialised fiscal term used solely by turnstile operatives at Regent's Park zoo. It refers to the variable amount of increase in the gate takings on a Sunday afternoon, caused by persons going to the zoo because they are in love and believe that the feeling of romance will be somehow enhanced by the smell of panther sweat and rank incontinence in the reptile house.

DUNBOYNE (n.)
The moment of realisation that the train you have just patiently watched pulling out of the station was the one you were meant to be on.

DUNCRAGGON (n.)
The name of Charles Bronson's retirement cottage.

DUNGENESS (n.)
The uneasy feeling that the plastic handles of the overloaded supermarket carrier bag you are carrying are getting steadily longer.

DUNTISH (adj.)
Mentally incapacitated by a severe hangover.

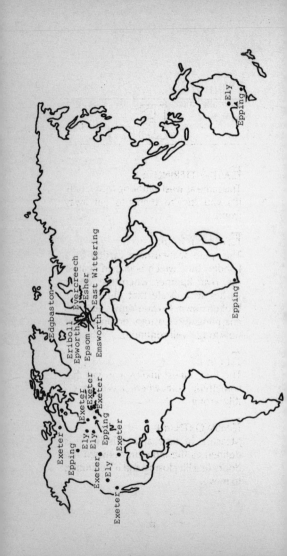

E

EAST WITTERING (n.)
The same as west wittering (q.v.), only it's you they're trying to get away from.

EDGBASTON (n.)
The spare seat-cushion carried by a London bus, which is placed against the rear bumper when the driver wishes to indicate that the bus has broken down. No one knows how this charming old custom originated or how long it will continue.

ELY (n.)
The first, tiniest inkling you get that something, somewhere, has gone teribly wrong.

EMSWORTH (n.)
Measure of time and noiselessness defined as the moment between the doors of a lift closing and it beginning to move.

EPPING (participial vb.)
The futile movements of forefingers and eyebrows used when failing to attract the attention of waiters and barmen.

EPSOM (n.)
An entry in a diary (such as a date or a set of initials) or a name and address in your address book, which you haven't the faintest idea what it's doing there.

EPWORTH (n.)
The precise value of the usefulness of epping (q.v.). It is a little-known fact that an earlier draft of the final line of the film *Gone with the Wind* had Clark Gable saying, 'Frankly my dear, I don't give an epworth', the line being eventually changed on the grounds that it might not be understood in Cleveland.

ERIBOLL (n.)
A brown bubble of cheese containing gaseous matter which grows on welsh rarebit. It was Sir Alexander Fleming's study of eribolls which led, indirectly, to his discovery of the fact that he didn't like welsh rarebit very much.

Esher (n.)
One of those push taps installed in public washrooms enabling the user to wash their trousers without actually getting into the basin. The most powerful esher of recent years was 'damped down' by Red Adair after an incredible sixty-eight days' fight in Manchester's Piccadilly Station.

Evercreech (n.)
The look given by a group of polite, angry people to a rude, calm queue-barger.

Ewelme (n., vb.)
The smile bestowed on you by an air hostess.

Exeter (n.)
All light household and electrical goods contain a number of vital components plus at least one exeter.

   If you've just mended a fuse, changed a bulb or fixed a blender, the exeter is the small, flat or round plastic or bakelite piece left over which means you have to undo everything and start all over again.

F

FAIRYMOUNT (vb., n.)
Polite word for buggery.

FARDUCKMANTON (n. archaic)
An ancient edict, mysteriously omitted from the Domesday Book, requiring that the feeding of fowl on village ponds should be carried out equitably.

FARNHAM (n.)
The feeling you get at about four o'clock in the afternoon when you haven't got enough done.

FARRANCASSIDY (n.)
A long and ultimately unsuccessful attempt to undo someone's bra.

FEAKLE (vb.)
To make facial expressions similar to those that old gentlemen make to young girls in the playground.

Finuge (vb.)
In any division of foodstuffs equally between several people, to give yourself the extra slice left over.

Fiunary (n.)
The safe place you put something and then forget where it was.

Flimby (n.)
One of those irritating handle-less slippery translucent plastic bags you get in supermarkets which, no matter how you hold them, always contrive to let something fall out.

Flodigarry (n. Scots)
An ankle-length gaberdine or oilskin tarpaulin worn by deep-sea herring fishermen in Arbroath and publicans in Glasgow.

Foindle (vb.)
To queue-jump very discreetly by working one's way up the line without being spotted doing so.

Forsinain (n. archaic)
The right of the lord of the manor to molest dwarves on their birthdays.

FOVANT (n.)
A taxi driver's gesture, a raised hand pointed out of the window which purports to mean 'thank you' and actually means 'fuck off out of my way'.

FRADDAM (n.)
The small awkward-shaped piece of cheese which remains after grating a large regular-shaped piece of cheese and enables you to cut your fingers.

FRAMLINGHAM (n.)
A kind of burglar alarm in common usage. It is cunningly designed so that it can ring at full volume in the street without apparently disturbing anyone.

Other types of framlinghams are burglar alarms fitted to business premises in residential areas, which go off as a matter of regular routine at 5.31 p.m. on a Friday evening and do not get turned off till 9.20 a.m. on Monday morning.

Frant (n.)
Measure. The legal minimum distance between two trains on the District and Circle lines of the London Underground. A frant, which must be not less than 122 chains (or 8 leagues) long, is not connected in any way with the adjective 'frantic' which comes to us by a completely different route (as indeed do the trains).

Frating Green (adj.)
The shade of green which is supposed to make you feel comfortable in hospitals, industrious in schools and uneasy in police stations.

Frimley (n.)
Exaggerated carefree saunter adopted by Norman Wisdom as an immediate prelude to dropping down an open manhole.

Fring (n.)
The noise made by a light bulb which has just shone its last.

FROLESWORTH (n.)
Measure. The minimum time it is necessary to spend frowning in deep concentration at each picture in an art gallery in order that everyone else doesn't think you're a complete moron.

FROSSES (pl. n.)
The lecherous looks exchanged between sixteen-year-olds at a party given by someone's parents.

FULKING (participial vb.)
Pretending not to be in when the carol-singers come round.

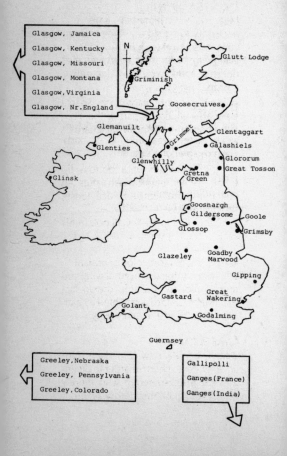

Glasgow, Jamaica
Glasgow, Kentucky
Glasgow, Missouri
Glasgow, Montana
Glasgow, Virginia
Glasgow, Nr.England

N

Griminish

Glutt Lodge

Goosecruives

Glemanuilt
Grimmet
Glentaggart

Glenties
Galashiels

Glenwhilly
Glororum

Great Tosson

Gretna
Green

Glinsk

Goosnargh
Gildersome
Goole

Glossop
Grimsby

Glazeley
Goadby
Marwood

Gipping

Gastard
Great
Wakering

Golant
Godalming

Guernsey

Greeley, Nebraska
Greeley, Pennsylvania
Greeley, Colorado

Gallipolli
Ganges (France)
Ganges (India)

G

GALASHIELS (pl. n.)
A form of particularly long sparse sideburns which are part of the mandatory uniform of British Rail guards.

GALLIPOLI (adj.)
Of the behaviour of a bottom lip trying to spit mouthwash after an injection at the dentist. Hence, loose, floppy, useless.

'She went suddenly Gallipoli in his arms' – Noel Coward.

GANGES (n. rare: colonial Indian)
Leg-rash contracted from playing too much polo. (It is a little-known fact that Prince Charles is troubled by ganges down the inside of his arms.)

GASTARD (n.)
Useful specially new-coined word for an illegitimate child (in order to distinguish it from someone who merely carves you up on the motorway, etc.).

GILDERSOME (adj.)
Descriptive of a joke someone tells you which starts well, but which becomes so embellished in the telling that you start to weary of it after scarcely half an hour.

GIPPING (participial vb.)
The fish-like opening and closing of the jaws seen amongst people who have recently been to the dentist and are puzzled as to whether their teeth have been put back the right way up.

GLASGOW (n.)
The feeling of infinite sadness engendered when walking through a place filled with happy people fifteen years younger than yourself.

GLASSEL (n.)
A seaside pebble which was shiny and interesting when wet, and which is now a lump of rock, which children nevertheless insist on filling their suitcases with after the holiday.

GLAZELEY (adj.)
The state of a barrister's flat greasy hair after wearing a wig all day.

GLEMANUILT (n.)
The kind of guilt which you'd completely forgotten about which comes roaring back on discovering an old letter in a cupboard.

GLENTAGGART (n.)
A particular kind of tartan hold-all, made exclusively under licence for British Airways.

When waiting to collect your luggage from an airport conveyor belt, you will notice that on the next conveyor belt along there is always a single, solitary bag going round and round uncollected. This is a glentaggart, which has been placed there by the baggage-handling staff to take your mind off the fact that your own luggage will shortly be landing in Murmansk.

GLENTIES (pl. n.)
Series of small steps by which someone who has made a serious tactical error in a conversation or argument moves from complete disagreement to wholehearted agreement.

GLENWHILLY (n. Scots)
A small tartan pouch worn beneath the kilt during the thistle-harvest.

GLINSK (n.)
A hat which politicians buy to go to Russia in.

GLORORUM (n.)
One who takes pleasure in informing others about their bowel movements.

GLOSSOP (n.)
A rogue blob of food.

Glossops, which are generally steaming hot and highly adhesive, invariably fall off your spoon and on to the surface of your host's highly polished antique-rosewood dining table. If this has not, or may not have, been noticed by the company present, swanage (q.v.) may be employed.

GLUTT LODGE (n.)
The place where food can be stored after having a tooth extracted. Some Arabs can go without sustenance for up to six weeks on a full glutt lodge, hence the expression 'the shit of the dessert'.

GOADBY MARWOOD (n.)
Someone who stops John Cleese on the street and demands that he does a funny walk.

GODALMING (n.)
Wonderful rush of relief on discovering that the ely (q.v.) and the wembley (q.v.) were in fact false alarms.

GOLANT (adj.)
Blank, sly, and faintly embarrassed. Pertaining to the expression seen on the face of someone who has clearly forgotten your name.

GOOLE (n.)
The puddle on the bar into which the barman puts your change.

GOOSECRUIVES (pl. n. archaic)
A pair of wooden trousers worn by poultry-keepers in the Middle Ages.

GOOSNARGH (n.)
Something left over from preparing or eating a meal, which you store in the fridge despite the fact that you know full well you will never ever use it.

GREAT TOSSON (n.)
A fat book containing four words and six cartoons which costs £6.95.

GREAT WAKERING (participial vb.)
Panic which sets in when you badly need to go to the lavatory and cannot make up your mind about what book or magazine to take with you.

GREELEY (n.)
Someone who continually annoys you by continually apologising for annoying you.

GRETNA GREEN (adj.)
A shade of green which makes you wish you'd painted whatever it was a different colour.

GRIMMET (n.)
A small bush from which cartoon characters dangle over the edge of a cliff.

GRIMSBY (n.)
A lump of something gristly and foul-tasting concealed in a mouthful of stew or pie.

Grimsbies are sometimes merely the result of careless cookery, but more often they are placed there deliberately by Freemasons. Grimsbies can be purchased in bulk from any respectable Masonic butcher on giving him the secret Masonic handbag. One is then placed in a guest's food to see if he knows the correct masonic method of dealing with it. If the guest is not a Mason, the host may find it entertaining to watch how he handles the obnoxious object. It may be

(a) manfully swallowed, invariably bringing tears to the eyes,

(b) chewed with resolution for up to twenty minutes before eventually resorting to method (a),

(c) choked on fatally.

The Masonic handshake is easily recognised by another Mason, incidentally, for by it a used grimsby is passed from hand to hand.

The secret Masonic method for dealing with a grimsby is as follows: remove it carefully with the silver tongs provided, using the left hand. Cross the room to your host, hopping on one leg, and ram the grimsby firmly up his nose, shouting, 'Take that, you smug Masonic bastard.'

GRINSTEAD (n.)
The state of a lady's clothing after she has been to powder her nose and has hitched up her tights over her skirt at the back, thus exposing her bottom, and has walked out without noticing it.

GUERNSEY (adj.)
Queasy but unbowed. The kind of feeling one gets when discovering a plastic compartment in a fridge in which things are growing.

GWEEK (n.)
A coat hanger recycled as a car aerial.

Hadzor (n.)
A sharp instrument placed in the washing-up bowl which makes it easier to cut yourself.

Hagnaby (n.)
Someone who looked a lot more attractive in the disco than they do in your bed the next morning.

Halcro (n.)
An adhesive fibrous cloth used to hold babies' clothes together. Thousands of tiny pieces of jam 'hook' on to thousands of tiny pieces of dribble, enabling the cloth to become 'sticky'.

Halifax (n.)
The green synthetic astroturf on which greengrocers display their vegetables.

N

Huna
Halcro

Hutlerburn
Harbottle

Hoff
Hunsingore
Huttoft
Hoddlesden   Huby   Haxby   Hull
Halifax
Hoylake   Hathersage   Humber
Hodnet   Hassop   Haugham
Hucknall   Hagnaby
Hadzor   Humby   Hickling
Hidcote
Bartram   Hoggeston   Harpenden
Heanton Punchardon   Hobbs Cross
Henstridge   Hever   Harbledown
Hastings
Hambledown   Herstmonceux
Haselbury
Plucknett

Hambledon (n.)
The sound of a single-engined aircraft flying by, heard whilst lying in a summer field in England, which somehow concentrates the silence and sense of space and timelessness and leaves one with a profound feeling of something or other.

Happle (vb.)
To annoy people by finishing their sentences for them and then telling them what they really meant to say.

Harbledown (vb.)
To manoeuvre a double mattress down a winding staircase.

Harbottle (n.)
A particular kind of fly which lives inside double glazing.

Harpenden (n.)
The coda to a phone conversation, consisting of about eight exchanges, by which people try gracefully to get off the line.

Haselbury Plucknett (n.)
A mechanical device for cleaning combs invented during the industrial revolution at the same time as Arkwright's Spinning Jenny, but which didn't catch on in the same way.

Hassop (n.)
The pocket down the back of an armchair used for storing two-shilling bits and pieces of Lego.

Hastings (pl. n.)
Things said on the spur of the moment to explain to someone who comes into a room unexpectedly precisely what it is you are doing.

Hathersage (n.)
The tiny snippets of beard which coat the inside of a washbasin after shaving in it.

Haugham (n.)
One who loudly informs other diners in a restaurant what kind of man he is by calling for the chef by his christian name from the lobby.

Haxby (n.)
Any garden implement found in a potting shed whose exact purpose is unclear.

Heanton Punchardon (n.)
A violent argument which breaks out in the car on the way home from a party between a couple who have had to be polite to each other in company all evening.

Henstridge (n.)
The dried yellow substance found between the prongs of forks in restaurants.

Herstmonceux (n.)
The correct name for the gold medallion worn by someone who is in the habit of wearing their shirt open to the waist.

Hever (n.)
The panic caused by half-hearing a Tannoy in an airport.

Hibbing (n.)
The marks left on the outside breast pocket of a storekeeper's overall where he has put away his pen and missed.

HICKLING (participial vb.)
The practice of infuriating theatre-goers by not only arriving late to a centre-row seat, but also loudly apologising to and patting each member of the audience in turn.

HIDCOTE BARTRAM (n.)
To be caught in a hidcote bartram is to say a series of protracted and final goodbyes to a group of people, leave the house and then realise you've left your hat behind.

HIGH LIMERIGG (n.)
The topmost tread of a staircase which disappears when you're climbing the stairs in the darkness.

HIGH OFFLEY (n.)
Goosnargh (q.v.) three weeks later.

HOBBS CROSS (n.)
The awkward leaping manoeuvre a girl has to go through in bed in order to make him sleep on the wet patch.

HODDLESDEN (n.)
An 'injured' footballer's limp back into the game which draws applause but doesn't fool anybody.

HODNET (n.)
The wooden safety platform supported by scaffolding round a building under construction from which the builders (at almost no personal risk) can drop pieces of cement on passers-by.

HOFF (vb.)
To deny indignantly something which is palpably true.

HOGGESTON (n.)
The action of overshaking a pair of dice in a cup in the mistaken belief that this will affect the eventual outcome in your favour and not irritate everyone else.

HORTON-CUM-STUDLEY (n.)
The combination of little helpful grunts, nodding movements of the head, considerate smiles, upward frowns and serious pauses that a group of people join in making in trying to elicit the next pronouncement of somebody with a dreadful stutter.

Hove (adj.)
Descriptive of the expression seen on the face of one person in the presence of another who clearly isn't going to stop talking for a very long time.

Hoylake (n.)
The pool of edible gravy which surrounds an inedible and disgusting lump of meat – eaten to give the impression that the person is 'just not very hungry, but mmm this is delicious'.

Cf. PEASLAKE – a similar experience had by vegetarians.

Huby (n.)
A half-erection large enough to be a publicly embarrassing bulge in the trousers, not large enough to be of any use to anybody.

Hucknall (vb.)
To crouch upwards: as in the movement of a seated person's feet and legs made in order to allow a cleaner's hoover to pass beneath them.

Hull (adj.)
Descriptive of the smell of a weekend cottage.

Humber (vb.)
To move like the cheeks of a very fat person as their car goes over a cattle grid.

Humby (n.)
An erection which won't go down when a gentleman has to go for a pee in the middle of making love to someone.

Huna (n.)
The result of coming to the wrong decision.

Hunsingore (n.)
Medieval ceremonial brass horn with which the successful execution of an araglin (q.v.) is trumpeted from the castle battlements.

Hutlerburn (n. archaic)
A burn sustained as a result of the behaviour of a clumsy hutler. (The precise duties of hutlers are now lost in the mists of history.)

Huttoft (n.)
The fibrous algae which grows in the dark, moist environment of trouser turn-ups.

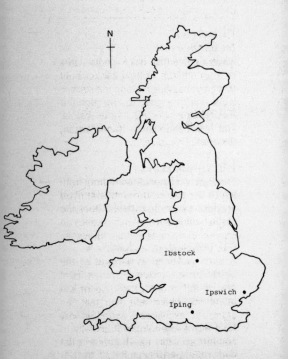

I

IBSTOCK (n.)
Anything used to make a noise on a corrugated iron wall or clinker-built fence by dragging it along the surface while walking past it. 'Mr Bennett thoughtfully selected a stout ibstock and left the house.' – Jane Austen, *Pride and Prejudice*, II.

IPING (participial vb.)
The increasingly anxious shifting from leg to leg you go through when you are desperate to go to the lavatory and the person you are talking to keeps on remembering a few final things he wants to mention.

IPSWICH (n.)
The sound at the other end of the telephone which tells you that the automatic exchange is working very hard but is intending not actually to connect you this time, merely to let you know how difficult it is.

N

Jawcraig
•

Jurby

Jarrow
•

J

JARROW (adj.)
An agricultural device which, when towed behind a tractor, enables the farmer to spread his dung evenly across the width of the road.

JAWCRAIG (n. medical)
A massive facial spasm which is brought on by being told a really astounding piece of news.

   A mysterious attack of jawcraig affected 40,000 sheep in Wales in 1952.

JURBY (n.)
A loose woollen garment reaching to the knees and with three or more armholes, knitted by the wearer's well-meaning but incompetent aunt.

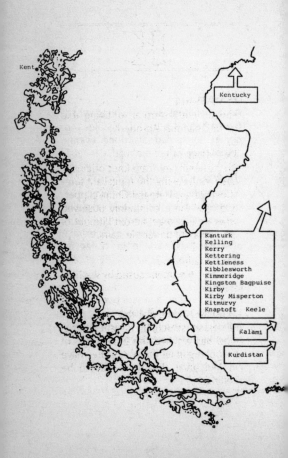

Kent

Kentucky

Kanturk
Kelling
Kerry
Kettering
Kettleness
Kibblesworth
Kimmeridge
Kingston Bagpuise
Kirby
Kirby Misperton
Kitmurvy
Knaptoft   Keele

Kalami

Kurdistan

KALAMI (n.)
The ancient Eastern art of being able to fold road-maps properly.

KANTURK (n.)
An extremely intricate knot originally used for belaying the topgallant fore-sheets of a gaff-rigged China clipper, and now more commonly observed when trying to get an old kite out of the cupboard under the stairs.

KEELE (adj.)
The horrible smell caused by washing ashtrays.

KELLING (participial vb.)
A person searching for something, who has reached the futile stage of re-looking in all the places they have looked once already, is said to be kelling.

Kent (adj.)
Politely determined not to help despite a violent urge to the contrary.

Kent expressions are seen on the faces of people who are good at something watching someone else who can't do it at all.

Kentucky (adv.)
Fitting exactly and satisfyingly.

The cardboard box that slides neatly into an exact space in a garage, or the last book which exactly fills a bookshelf, is said to fit 'real nice and kentucky'.

Kerry (n.)
The small twist of skin which separates each sausage on a string.

Kettering (n.)
The marks left on your bottom or thighs after sunbathing on a wickerwork chair.

Kettleness (adj.)
The quality of not being able to pee while being watched.

Kibblesworth (n.)
The footling amount of money by which the price of a given article in a

shop is less than a sensible number, in the vain hope that at least one idiot will think it cheap. For instance, the kibblesworth on a pair of shoes priced at £19.99 is 1p.

KIMMERIDGE (n.)
The light breeze which blows through your armpit hair when you are stretched out sunbathing.

KINGSTON BAGPUISE (n.)
A forty-year-old sixteen-stone man trying to commit suicide by jogging.

KIRBY (n.)
Small but repulsive piece of food prominently attached to a person's face or clothing.
See also CHIPPING ONGAR.

KIRBY MISPERTON (n.)
One who kindly attempts to wipe an apparent kirby (q.v.) off another's face with a napkin, and then discovers it to be a wart or other permanent fixture, is said to have committed a 'kirby misperton'.

KITMURVY (n.)
Man who owns all the latest sporting gadgetry and clothing (golf trolley, tee cosies, ventilated shoes, Gary Player-autographed tracksuit top, American navy cap, mirror sunglasses) but is still only on his second golf lesson.

KNAPTOFT (n.)
The mysterious fluff placed in your pockets by dry-cleaning firms.

KURDISTAN (n.)
Hard stare given by a husband to his wife when he notices a sharp increase in the number of times he answers the phone to be told, 'Sorry, wrong number.'

L

LAMLASH (n.)
The folder on hotel dressing-tables full of astoundingly dull information.

LARGOWARD (n.)
Motorists' name for the kind of pedestrian who stands beside a main road and waves on the traffic, as if it's their right of way.

LE TOUQUET (n.)
A mere nothing, an unconsidered trifle, a negligible amount. Un touquet is often defined as the difference between the cost of a bottle of gin bought in an off-licence and one bought in a duty-free shop.

LIFF (n.)
A book, the contents of which are totally belied by its cover. For instance, any book the dust jacket of which bears the words 'This book will change your life.'

N

Lubcroy •   • Lybster
          • Lossiemouth

       • Liff
 Limerigg   • Largoward
Lochranza   • Luffness
    • Lamlash   • Longniddry
       • Lindisfarne

       Low
Louth •   Ardwell   • Lowther
   Little Urswick

• Listowel

      • Lower Peover
           • Lusby
   Llanelli •   • Ludlow
              • Lowestoft
     Lydiard
     Tregoze   • Luton
    • Luppitt
     Lulworth

          Le Touquet •

LIMERIGG (vb.)
To jar one's leg as the result of the disappearance of a stair which isn't there in the darkness.

LINDISFARNE (adj.)
Descriptive of the pleasant smell of an empty biscuit tin.

LISTOWEL (n.)
The small mat on the bar designed to be more absorbent than the bar, but not as absorbent as your elbows.

LITTLE URSWICK (n.)
The member of any class who most inclines a teacher towards the view that capital punishment should be introduced in schools.

LLANELLI (adj.)
Descriptive of the waggling movement of a person's hands when shaking water from them or warming up for a piece of workshop theatre.

LOCHRANZA (n.)
The long unaccompanied wail in the middle of a Scottish folk song where the pipers nip round the corner for a couple of drinks.

LONGNIDDRY (n.)
A droplet which persists in running out of your nose.

LOSSIEMOUTH (n.)
One of those middle-aged ladies with just a hint of a luxuriant handlebar moustache.

LOUTH (n.)
The sort of man who wears loud check jackets, has a personalised tankard behind the bar and always gets served before you do.

LOW ARDWELLO (n.)
Seductive remark made hopefully in the back of a taxi.

LOW EGGBOROUGH (n.)
A quiet little unregarded man in glasses who is building a new kind of atomic bomb in his garden shed.

LOWER PEOVER (n.)
Common solution to the problem of a humby (q.v.)

LOWESTOFT (n.)
(a) The balls of wool which collect on nice new sweaters.
(b) The correct name for 'navel fluff'.

LOWTHER (vb.)
(Of a large group of people who have been to the cinema together.) To stand aimlessly about on the pavement and argue about whether to go and eat either a Chinese meal nearby or an Indian meal at a restaurant which somebody says is very good but isn't certain where it is, or have a drink and think about it, or just go home, or have a Chinese meal nearby – until by the time agreement is reached everything is shut.

LUBCROY (n.)
The telltale little lump in the top of your swimming trunks which tells you you are going to have to spend half an hour with a safety pin trying to pull the drawstring out again.

LUDLOW (n.)
A wad of newspaper, folded table-napkin or lump of cardboard put under a wobbly table or chair to make it stand up straight.

It is perhaps not widely known that air-ace Sir Douglas Bader used to get about on an enormous pair of ludlows before he had his artificial legs fitted.

LUFFENHAM (n.)
Feeling you get when the pubs aren't going to be open for another forty-five minutes and the luffness is beginning to wear a bit thin.

LUFFNESS (n.)
Hearty feeling that comes from walking on the moors with gumboots and cold ears.

LULWORTH (n.)
Measure of conversation.

A lulworth defines the amount of the length, loudness and embarrassment of a statement you make when everyone else in the room unaccountably stops talking at the same moment.

LUPPITT (n.)
The piece of leather which hangs off the bottom of your shoe before you can be bothered to get it mended.

LUSBY (n.)
The fold of flesh pushing forward over the top of a bra which is too small for the lady inside it.

Luton (n.)
The horseshoe-shaped rug which goes round a lavatory seat.

Lybster (n., vb.)
The artificial chuckle in the voice-over at the end of a supposedly funny television commercial.

Lydiard Tregoze (n.)
The opposite of a mavis enderby (q.v.). An unrequited early love of your life who still causes terrible pangs though she inexplicably married a telephone engineer.

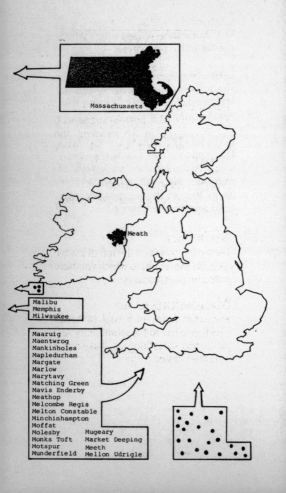

Massachussets

Meath

Malibu
Memphis
Milwaukee

Maaruig
Maentwrog
Mankinholes
Mapledurham
Margate
Marlow
Marytavy
Matching Green
Mavis Enderby
Meathop
Melcombe Regis
Melton Constable
Minchinhampton
Moffat
Molesby   Mugeary
Monks Toft   Market Deeping
Motspur   Meeth
Munderfield   Mellon Udrigle

M

Maaruig (n.)
The inexpressible horror experienced on waking up in the morning and remembering that you are Andy - Stewart.

Maentwrog (n. Welsh)
Celtic word for a computer spelling mistake.

Malibu (n.)
The height by which the top of a wave exceeds the height to which you have rolled up your trousers.

Mankinholes (pl. n.)
The small holes in a loaf of bread which give rise to the momentary suspicion that something may have made its home within.

Mapledurham (n.)
A hideous piece of chipboard veneer furniture bought in a suburban high-street furniture store and designed to hold exactly a year's supply of Sunday colour supplements.

Margate (n.)
A margate is a particular kind of commissionaire who sees you every day and is on cheerful Christian-name terms with you, then one day refuses to let you in because you've forgotten your identity card.

Market Deeping (participial vb.)
Stealing one piece of fruit from a street fruit-and-vegetable stall.

Marlow (n.)
The bottom drawer in the kitchen your mother keeps her paper bags in.

Marytavy (n.)
A person to whom, under dire injunctions of silence, you tell a secret which you wish to be far more widely known.

Massachusetts (pl. n.)
Those items and particles which people who, after blowing their noses, are searching for when they look into their hankies.

Matching Green (adj.)
(Of neckties.) Any colour which Nigel Rees rejects as unsuitable for his trousers or jacket.

Mavis Enderby (n.)
The almost-completely-forgotten girl-friend from your distant past for whom your wife has a completely irrational jealousy and hatred.

Meath (adj.)
Warm and very slightly clammy.

Descriptive of the texture of your hands after the automatic drying machine has turned itself off, just damp enough to make it embarrassing if you have to shake hands with someone immediately afterwards.

Meathop (n.)
One who sets off for the scene of an aircraft crash with a picnic hamper.

MEETH (n.)
Something which American doctors will shortly tell us we are all suffering from.

MELCOMBE REGIS (n.)
The name of the style of decoration used in cocktail lounges in mock-Tudor hotels in Surrey.

MELLON UDRIGLE (n.)
The ghastly sound made by traditional folk-singers.

MELTON CONSTABLE (n.)
A patent anti-wrinkle cream which policemen wear to keep themselves looking young.

MEMPHIS (n.)
The little bits of yellow fluff which get trapped in the hinge of the wind-screen wipers after polishing the car with a new duster.

Milwaukee (n.)
The melodious whistling, chanting and humming tone of the milwaukee can be heard whenever a public lavatory is entered. It is the way the occupants of the cubicles have of telling you there's no lock on their door and you can't come in.

Minchinhampton (n.)
The expression on a man's face when he has just zipped up his trousers without due care and attention.

Moffat (n. tailoring term)
That part of your coat which is designed to be sat on by the person next to you on the bus.

Molesby (n.)
The kind of family that drives to the seaside and then sits in the car with all the windows closed, reading the *Sunday Express* and wearing sidcups (q.v.).

Monks Toft (n.)
The bundle of hair which is left after a monk has been tonsured, which he keeps tied up with a rubber band and uses for chasing ants away.

Motspur (n.)
The fourth wheel of a supermarket trolley which looks identical to the other three but renders the trolley completely uncontrollable.

Mugeary (n. medical)
The substance from which the unpleasant little yellow globules in the corners of a sleepy person's eyes are made.

Munderfield (n.)
A meadow selected, whilst driving past, as being ideal for a picnic which, from a sitting position, turns out to be full of stubble, dust and cowpats, and almost impossible to enjoy yourself in.

N

NAAS (n.)
The winemaking region of Albania where most of the wine that people take to bottle-parties comes from.

NACTON (n.)
The *'n'* with which cheap advertising copywriters replace the word 'and' (as in 'fish 'n' chips', 'mix 'n' match', 'assault 'n' battery'), in the mistaken belief that this is in some way chummy or endearing.

NAD (n.)
Measure defined as the distance between a driver's outstretched fingertips and the ticket machine in an automatic car-park.
  1 nad = 18.4 cm.

N

Nubbock

Naas

Nad

Nanhoron

Nether
Poppleton

Nantwich

Neen
Sollars

Naseby

Nottage

Nazeing

Nacton

Nempnett
Thrubwell

Nutbourne

Nantucket
Naugatuck

Naples

Nybster

Nanhoron (n. medical)
A tiny valve concealed in the inner ear which enables a deaf grandmother to converse quite normally when she feels like it, but which excludes completely anything that sounds like a request to help with laying the table.

Nantucket (n.)
The secret pocket which eats your train ticket.

Nantwich (n.)
A late-night snack, invented by the Earl of Nantwich, which consists of the dampest thing in the fridge, pressed between two of the driest things in the fridge. The Earl, who lived in a flat in Clapham, invented the nantwich to avoid having to go shopping.

Naples (pl. n.)
The tiny depressions in a piece of Ryvita.

Naseby (n.)
The stout metal instrument used for clipping labels on to exhibits at flower shows.

Naugatuck (n.)
A plastic sachet containing shampoo, polyfilla, etc., which is impossible to open except by biting off the corners.

Nazeing (participial vb.)
The rather unconvincing noises of pretended interest which an adult has to make when brought a small dull object for admiration by a child.

Neen Sollars (pl. n.)
Any ensemble of especially unflattering and peculiar garments worn by a woman which tell you that she is right at the forefront of fashion.

Nempnett Thrubwell (n.)
The feeling experienced when driving off for the first time on a brand new motorbike.

Nether Poppleton (n. obs.)
A pair of P. J. Proby's trousers.

Nottage (n.)
Nottage is the collective name for things which you find a use for immediately after you've thrown them away.

For instance, your greenhouse has been cluttered up for years with a huge piece of cardboard and great fronds of gardening string. You at last decide to clear all this stuff out, and you burn it. Within twenty-four hours you will urgently need to wrap a large parcel, and suddenly remember that luckily in your greenhouse there is some cardb . . .

NUBBOCK (n.)
The kind of person who has to leave before a party can relax and enjoy itself.

NUTBOURNE (n.)
In a choice between two or more possible puddings, the one nobody plumps for.

NYBSTER (n.)
Sort of person who takes the lift to travel one floor.

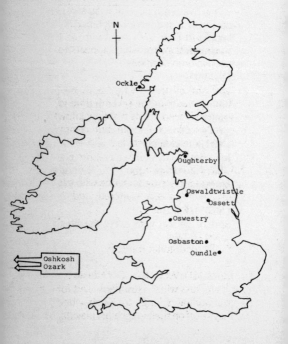

OCKLE (n.)
An electrical switch which appears to be off in both positions.

OSBASTON (n.)
A point made for the seventh time to somebody who insists that they know exactly what you mean but clearly hasn't got the faintest idea.

OSHKOSH (n., vb.)
The noise made by someone who has just been grossly flattered and is trying to make light of it.

OSSETT (n.)
A frilly spare-toilet-roll-cosy.

OSWALDTWISTLE (n. Old Norse)
Small brass wind instrument used for summoning Vikings to lunch when they're off on their longships, playing.

OSWESTRY (abs. n.)
Bloody-minded determination on part of a storyteller to continue a story which both the teller and the listeners know has become desperately tedious.

OUGHTERBY (n.)
Someone you don't want to invite to a party but whom you know you have to as a matter of duty.

OUNDLE (vb.)
To walk along leaning sideways, with one arm hanging limp and dragging one leg behind the other.

Most commonly used by actors in amateur productions of *Richard III*, or by people carrying a heavy suitcase in one hand.

OZARK (n.)
One who offers to help just after all the work has been done.

P

PABBAY (n., vb.)
(Fencing term.) The play, or manoeuvre, where one swordsman leaps
on to the table and pulls the battleaxe
off the wall.

PANT-Y-WACCO (adj.)
The final state of mind of a retired
colonel before they come to take him
away.

PAPCASTLE (n.)
Something drawn or modelled by a
small child which you are supposed to
know what it is.

PAPPLE (vb.)
To do what babies do to soup with
their spoons.

PAPWORTH EVERARD (n.)
Technical term for the third take of an
orgasm scene during the making of a
pornographic film.

PEEBLES (pl. n.)
Small, carefully rolled pellets of skegness (q.v.).

PELUTHO (n.)
A South American ball game. The balls are whacked against a brick wall with a stout wooden bat until the prisoner confesses.

PENGE (n.)
The expanding slotted arm on which a cuckoo comes out of a cuckoo clock.

PEN TRE-TAFARN-Y-FEDW (n.)
Welsh word which literally translates as 'leaking-biro-by-the-glass-hole-of-the-clerk-of-the-bank-has-been-taken-to-another-place-leaving-only-the-special-inkwell-and-three-inches-of-tin-chain'.

PEORIA (n.)
The fear of peeling too few potatoes.

PERCYHORNER (n.)
(English public-school slang.) A prefect whose duty it is to surprise new boys at the urinal and humiliate them in a manner of his choosing.

Perranzabuloe (n.)
One of those spray things used to wet ironing with.

Pevensey (n. archaic)
The right to collect shingle from the king's foreshore.

Piddletrenthide (n.)
A trouser stain caused by a wimbledon (q.v.). Not to be confused with a botley (q.v.).

Pimlico (n.)
Small odd-shaped piece of plastic or curious metal component found in the bottom of kitchen rummage-drawer when spring-cleaning or looking for Sellotape.

Pimperne (n.)
One of those rubber nodules found on the underneath side of a lavatory seat.

Pitlochry (n.)
The background gurgling noise heard in Wimpy Bars caused by people trying to get the last bubbles out of their milkshakes by slurping loudly through their straws.

PITSLIGO (n.)
Part of traditional mating rite.

   During the first hot day of spring, all the men in the tube start giving up their seats to ladies and strap-hanging. The purpose of pitsligo is for them to demonstrate their manhood by displaying the wet patches under their arms.

PLEELEY (adj.)
Descriptive of a drunk person's attempts to be endearing.

PLYMOUTH (vb.)
To relate an amusing story to someone without remembering that it was they who told it to you in the first place.

PLYMPTON (n.)
The (pointless) knob on top of a war memorial.

PODE HOLE (n.)
A hole drilled in chipboard lavatory walls by homosexuals for any one of a number of purposes.

POGES (pl. n.)
The lumps of dry powder that remain after cooking a packet soup.

POLBATHIC (adj.)
Gifted with ability to manipulate taps using only the feet.

POLLOCH (n.)
One of those tiny ribbed-plastic and aluminium foil tubs of milk served on trains enabling you to carry one safely back to your compartment where you can spill the contents all over your legs in comfort trying to get the bloody thing open.

POLPERRO (n.)
A polperro is the ball, or muff, of soggy hair found clinging to bath overflow-holes.

POONA (n.)
Satisfied grunting noise made when sitting back after a good meal.

POTT SHRIGLEY (n.)
Dried remains of a week-old casserole, eaten when extremely drunk at two a.m.

PUDSEY (n.)
The curious-shaped flat wads of dough left on a kitchen table after someone has been cutting scones out of it.

QUABBS (pl. n.)
The substances which emerge when you squeeze a blackhead.

QUALL (vb.)
To speak with the voice of one who requires another to do something for them.

QUEDGELEY (n.)
A rabidly left-wing politician who can afford to be that way because he married a millionairess.

QUEENZIEBURN (n.)
Something that happens when people make it up after an agglethorpe (q.v.).

QUENBY (n.)
A stubborn spot on a window which you spend twenty minutes trying to clean off before discovering it's on the other side of the glass.

QUERRIN (n.)
A person that no one has ever heard of who unaccountably manages to make a living writing prefaces.

QUOYNESS (n.)
The hatefulness of words like 'relionus' and 'easiephit'.

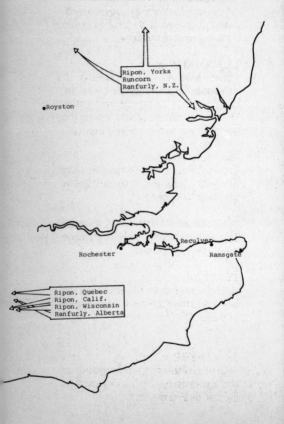

Ripon, Yorks
Runcorn
Ranfurly, N.Z.

•Royston

Reculver

Rochester   Ramsgate

Ripon, Quebec
Ripon, Calif.
Ripon, Wisconsin
Ranfurly, Alberta

RAMSGATE (n.)
All institutional buildings must, by
law, contain at least twenty ramsgates.
These are doors which open the
opposite way to the one you expect.

RANFURLY (adj.)
Fashion of tying ties so that the long
thin end underneath dangles below
the short fat upper end.

RECULVER (n.)
The sort of remark only ever made
during *Any Questions*.

RIPON (vb.)
(Of literary critics.) To include all the
best jokes from the book in the review
to make it look as if the critic thought
of them.

ROCHESTER (n.)
One who is able to gain occupation of
the armrests on both sides of their
cinema or aircraft seat.

Royston (n.)
The man behind you in church who sings with terrific gusto almost three quarters of a tone off the note.

Runcorn (n.)
A peeble (q.v.) which is larger than a belper (q.v.).

S

SADBERGE (n.)
A violent green shrub which is ground up, mixed with twigs and gelatine and served with clonmult (q.v.) and buldoo (q.v.) in a container referred to for no known reason as a 'relish tray'.

SAFFRON WALDEN (n.)
A particular kind of hideous casual jacket that nobody wears in real life, but which is much favoured by Ronnie Barker.

SATTERTHWAITE (vb.)
To spray the person you are talking to with half-chewed breadcrumbs or small pieces of whitebait.

SAVERNAKE (vb.)
To sew municipal crests on to a windcheater in the belief that this will make the wearer appear cosmopolitan.

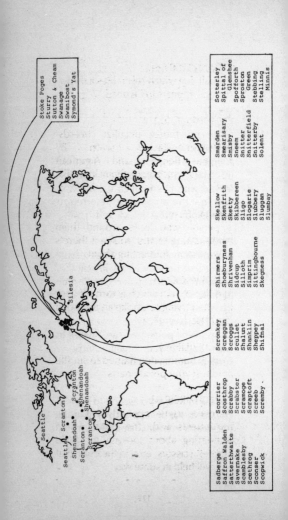

Seattle
Scranton
Scranton Shenandoah
Seattle Shenandoah
Scranton Shenandoah

Silesia

Stoke Poges
Sturry
Sutton & Cheam
Swanage
Swanibost
Symond's Yat

Sadberge	Scorrier	Shirmers	Skellow	Smarden	Sotterley
Saffron Walden	Scouthrop	Shoeburyness	Skenfrith	Smearisary	Spittal of Glenshee
Sawtry	Scrabby	Shrivenham	Sketty	Smisby	
Sawerthwaite	Scrabster	Sidcup	Skibbereen	Sneem	Spofforth
Seamlesby	Scramoge	Silloth	Sligo	Snitter	Sproston
Scethrog	Scraptoft	Simprim	Slogarie	Snitterfield	Green
Sconser	Screeb	Sittingbourne	Slubbery	Snitterby	Stebbing
Scopwick	Scremby	Skegness	Sluggan	Solent	Stelling
			Slumbay		Minnis

Scamblesby (n.)
A small dog which resembles a throw-rug and appears to be dead.

Scethrog (n.)
One of those peculiar beards-without-moustaches worn by religious Belgians and American scientists which help them look like trolls.

Sconser (n.)
A person who looks around them when talking to you, to see if there's anyone more interesting about.

Scopwick (n.)
The flap of skin which is torn off your lip when trying to smoke an untipped cigarette.

Scorrier (n.)
A small hunting dog trained to snuffle amongst your private parts.

Scosthrop (vb.)
To make vague opening or cutting movements with the hands when wandering about looking for a tin opener, scissors, etc., in the hope that this will help in some way.

SCRABBY (n.)
A curious-shaped duster given to you by your mother which on closer inspection turns out to be half an underpant.

SCRABSTER (n.)
One of those dogs which has it off on your leg during tea.

SCRAMOGE (vb.)
To cut oneself whilst licking envelopes.

SCRANTON (n.)
A person who, after the declaration of the bodmin (q.v.), always says, '. . . But I only had the tomato soup.'

SCRAPTOFT (n.)
The absurd flap of hair a vain and balding man grows long above one ear to comb it plastered over the top of his head to the other ear.

SCREEB (n.)
To make the noise of a nylon anorak rubbing against a pair of corduroy trousers.

SCREGGAN (n. banking)
The crossed-out bit caused by people putting the wrong year on their cheques all through January.

SCREMBY (n.)
The dehydrated felt-tip pen attached by a string to the 'Don't Forget' board in the kitchen which has never worked in living memory but which no one can be bothered to throw away.

SCROGGS (n.)
The stout pubic hairs which protrude from your helping of moussaka in a cheap Greek restaurant.

SCRONKEY (n.)
Something that hits the window as a result of a violent sneeze.

SCULLET (n.)
The last teaspoon in the washing up.

SEATTLE (vb.)
To make a noise like a train going along.

Shalunt (n.)
One who wears Trinidad and Tobago T-shirts on the beach in Bali to prove they didn't just win the holiday in a competition or anything.

Shanklin (n.)
The hoop of skin around a single slice of salami.

Shenandoah (n.)
The infinite smugness of one who knows they are entitled to a place in a nuclear bunker.

Sheppey (n.)
Measure of distance (equal to approximately seven eighths of a mile), defined as the closest distance at which sheep remain picturesque.

Shifnal (n., vb.)
An awkward shuffling walk caused by two or more people in a hurry accidentally getting into the same segment of a revolving door. A similar effect is achieved by people entering three-legged races unwisely joined at the neck instead of the ankles.

Shirmers (pl. n.)
Tall young men who stand around smiling at weddings as if to suggest that they know the bride rather well.

Shoeburyness (abs. n.)
The vague uncomfortable feeling you get when sitting on a seat which is still warm from somebody else's bottom.

Shrivenham (n.)
One of Germaine Greer's used-up lovers.

Sidcup (n.)
One of those hats made from tying knots in the corners of a handkerchief.

Silesia (n. medical)
The inability to remember, at the critical moment, which is the better side of a boat to be seasick off.

Silloth (n.)
Something that was sticky, and is now furry, found on the carpet under the sofa the morning after a party.

SIMPRIM (n.)
The little movement of false modesty by which a girl with a cavernous visible cleavage pulls her skirt down over her knees.

SITTINGBOURNE (n.)
One of those conversations where both people are waiting for the other one to shut up so they can get on with their bit.

SKEGNESS (n.)
Nose excreta of a malleable consistency.

SKELLOW (adj.)
Descriptive of the satisfaction experienced when looking at a really good dry-stone wall.

SKENFRITH (n.)
The flakes of athlete's foot found inside socks.

SKETTY (n.)
Apparently self-propelled little dance a beer glass performs in its own puddle.

Skibbereen (n.)
The noise made by a sunburned thigh leaving a plastic chair.

Sligo (n.)
An unnamed and exotic sexual act which people like to believe that famous film stars get up to in private. 'To commit sligo.'

Slogarie (n.)
Hillwalking dialect for the seven miles of concealed rough moorland which lie between what you thought was the top of the hill and what actually is.

Slubbery (n.)
The gooey drips of wax that dribble down the sides of a candle so beloved by Italian restaurants with Chianti bottles instead of wallpaper.

Sluggan (n.)
A lurid facial bruise which everyone politely omits to mention because it's obvious that you had a punch-up with your spouse last night – but which was actually caused by walking into a door. It is useless to volunteer the true explanation because nobody will believe it.

Slumbay (n.)
The cigarette end someone discovers in the mouthful of lager they have just swigged from a can at the end of a party.

Smarden (vb.)
To keep your mouth shut by smiling determinedly through your teeth. Smardening is largely used by people trying to give the impression that they're enjoying a story they've heard at least six times before.

Smearisary (n.)
That part of a kitchen wall reserved for the schooltime daubings of small children.

Smisby (n.)
The correct name for a junior apprentice greengrocer whose main duty is to arrange the fruit so that the bad side is underneath.

From the name of a character not in Dickens.

SNEEM (n., vb.)
Particular kind of frozen smile bestowed on a small child by a parent in mixed company when question, 'Mummy, what's this?' appears to require the answer, 'Er . . . it's a rubber johnny, darling.'

SNITTER (n.)
One of the rather unfunny newspaper clippings pinned to an office wall, the humour of which is supposed to derive from the fact that the headline contains a name similar to that of one of the occupants of the office.

SNITTERBY (n.)
Someone who pins snitters (q.v.) on to snitterfields (q.v.) and is also suspected of being responsible for the extinction of virginstows (q.v.).

SNITTERFIELD (n.)
Office noticeboard on which snitters (q.v.), cards saying 'You don't have to be mad to work here, but if you are it helps!!!' and slightly smutty postcards from Ibiza get pinned up by snitterbies (q.v.).

Solent (adj.)
Descriptive of the state of serene self-knowledge reached through drink.

Sotterley (n.)
Uncovered bit between two shops with awnings, which you have to cross when it's raining.

Spittal of Glenshee (n.)
That which has to be cleaned off castle floors in the morning after a bagpipe contest or vampire attack.

Spofforth (vb.)
To tidy up a room before the cleaning lady arrives.

Sproston Green (n.)
The violent colour of one of Nigel Rees's jackets, worn when he thinks he's being elegant.

Stebbing (n.)
The erection you cannot conceal because you're not wearing a jacket.

Stoke Poges (n.)

The tapping movements of an index finger on glass made by a person futilely attempting to communicate with *either* a tropical fish *or* a post office clerk.

Sturry (n., vb.)

A token run. Pedestrians who have chosen to cross a road immediately in front of an approaching vehicle generally give a little wave and break into a sturry. This gives the impression of hurrying without having any practical effect on their speed whatsoever.

Sutton and Cheam (nouns)

Sutton and cheam are the two kinds of dirt into which all dirt is divided. 'Sutton' is the dark sort that always gets on to light-coloured things, and 'cheam' the light-coloured sort that clings to dark items. Anyone who has ever found Marmite stains on a dress-shirt, or seagull goo on a dinner jacket (a) knows all about sutton and cheam, and (b) is going to some very curious dinner parties.

Swanage (pl. n.)

Swanage is the series of diversionary tactics used when trying to cover up the existence of a glossop (q.v.) and may include (a) uttering a high-pitched laugh and pointing out of the window (NB. this doesn't work more than twice); (b) sneezing as loudly as possible and wiping the glossop off the table in the same movement as whipping out your handkerchief; (c) saying 'Christ! I seem to have dropped some shit on your table' (very unwise); (d) saying 'Christ, who did that?' (better); (e) pressing your elbow on to the glossop itself and working your arms slowly to the edge of the table; (f) leaving the glossop where it is but moving a plate over it and putting up with sitting at an uncomfortable angle the rest of the meal; or, if the glossop is in too exposed a position, (g) leaving it there unremarked except for the occasional humorous glance.

SWANIBOST (adj.)
Complete shagged out after a hard day having income tax explained to you.

SYMOND'S YAT (n.)
The little spoonful inside the lid of a recently opened boiled egg.

T

TABLEY SUPERIOR (n.)
The look directed at you in a theatre bar in the interval by people who've already got their drinks.

TAMPA (n.)
The sound of a rubber eraser coming to rest after dropping off a desk in a very quiet room.

TAROOM (vb.)
To make loud noises during the night to let the burglars know you are in.

TEGUCIGALPA (n.)
An embarrassing mistake arising out of confusing the shape of something rather rude with something perfectly ordinary when groping for it in the darkness.

A common example of a tegucigalpa is when a woman pulls a packet of Tampax out of her bag and offers them around under the impression that it is a carton of cigarettes.

THEAKSTONE (n.)

Ancient mad tramp who jabbers to himself and swears loudly and obscenely on station platforms and traffic islands.

THROCKING (participial vb.)

The action of continually pushing down the lever on a pop-up toaster in the hope that you will thereby get it to understand that you want it to toast something.

Also: a style of drum-playing favoured by Nigel Olsson of the Elton John Band, reminiscent of the sound of someone slapping a frankfurter against a bucket. An excellent example of this is to be heard on 'Someone Saved My Life Tonight' from the album *Captain Fantastic and the Brown Dirt Cowboy*.

THROCKMORTON (n.)

The soul of a departed madman: one of those now known to inhabit the timing mechanism of pop-up toasters.

THRUMSTER (n.)

The irritating man next to you in a concert who thinks he's (a) the conductor, (b) the brass section.

THRUPP (vb.)
To hold a ruler on one end on a desk and make the other end go bbddbb-ddbbrrbrrrrddrr.

THURNBY (n.)
A rucked-up edge of carpet or linoleum which everyone says someone will trip over and break a leg unless it gets fixed. After a year or two someone trips over it and breaks a leg.

TIBSHELF (n.)
Criss-cross wooden construction hung on a wall in a teenage girl's bedroom which is covered with glass bambis and poodles, matching pigs and porcelain ponies in various postures.

TIDPIT (n.)
The corner of a toenail from which satisfying little black deposits may be sprung.

TIGHARRY (n.)
The accomplice or 'lure' who gets punters to participate in the three-card trick on London streets by winning an improbable amount of money very easily.

Tillicoultry (n.)
The man-to-man chumminess adopted by an employer as a prelude for telling an employee that he's going to have to let him go.

Timble (vb.)
(Of small nasty children.) To fall over very gently, look around to see who's about, and then yell blue murder.

Tincleton (n.)
A man who amuses himself in your lavatory by pulling the chain in mid-pee and then seeing if he can finish before the flush does.

Tingrith (n.)
The feeling of silver paper against your fillings.

Todber (n.)
One whose idea of a good time is to stand behind his front hedge and give surly nods to people he doesn't know.

Todding (vb.)
The business of talking amiably and aimlessly to the barman at the local.

Tolob (n.)
A crease or fold in an underblanket, the removal of which involves getting out of bed and largely remaking it.

Tolstachaolais (phr.)
What the police in Leith require you to say in order to prove that you are not drunk.

Tooting Bec (n.)
A car behind which one draws up at the traffic lights and hoots at when the lights go green before realising that the car is parked and there is no one inside.

Torlundy (n.)
Narrow but thickly grimed strip of floor between the fridge and the sink unit in the kitchen of a rented flat.

Toronto (n.)
Generic term for anything which comes out in a gush despite all your careful efforts to let it out gently, e.g. flour into a white sauce, tomato ketchup on to fried fish, sperm into a human being, etc.

TOTTERIDGE (n.)
The ridiculous two-inch hunch that people adopt when arriving late for the theatre in the vain and futile hope that it will minimise either the embarrassment of the lack of visibility for the rest of the audience.

Cf. hickling.

TRANTLEMORE (vb.)
To make a noise like a train crossing a set of points.

TREWOOFE (n.)
A very thick and heavy drift of snow balanced precariously on the edge of a door porch waiting for what it judges to be the correct moment to fall. From the ancient Greek legend 'The Trewoofe of Damocles'.

TRISPEN (n.)
A form of intelligent grass. It grows a single, tough stalk and makes its home on lawns. When it sees the lawnmower coming it lies down and pops up again after it has gone by.

TROSSACHS (pl. n.)
The useless epaulettes on an expensive raincoat.

TUAMGRANEY (n.)
A hideous wooden ornament that people hang over the mantelpiece to prove they've been to Africa.

TULSA (n.)
A slurp of beer which has accidentally gone down your shirt collar.

TUMBY (n.)
The involuntary abdominal gurgling which which fills the silence following someone else's intimate personal revelation.

TWEEDSMUIR (collective n.)
The name given to the extensive collection of hats kept in the downstairs lavatory which don't fit anyone in the family.

TWEMLOW GREEN (n.)
The colour of some of Nigel Rees's trousers, worn in the mistaken belief that they go rather well with his sproston green (q.v.) jacket.

TWOMILEBORRIS (n.)
A popular East European outdoor game in which the first person to reach the front of the meat queue wins, and the losers have to forfeit their bath plugs.

TYNE and WEAR (nouns)
The 'tyne' is the small priceless or vital object accidentally dropped on the floor (e.g. diamond tieclip, contact lens) and the 'wear' is the large immovable object (e.g. Welsh dresser, car-crusher) that it shelters under.

N

● Ullapool

● Ullock

Uttoxeter ●

● Ullingswick

● Umberleigh
● Upottery
● Upper
Beeding

ULLAPOOL (n.)
The spittle which builds up on the floor of the orchestra pit of the Royal Opera House.

ULLINGSWICK (n.)
An over-developed epiglottis found in middle-aged coloraturas.

ULLOCK (n.)
The correct name for either of the deaf Scandinavian tourists who are standing two abreast in front of you on the escalator.

UMBERLEIGH (n.)
The awful moment which follows a dorchester (q.v.) when a speaker weighs up whether to repeat an amusing remark after nobody laughed the last time. To be on the horns of an umberleigh is to wonder whether people didn't hear the remark, or whether they did hear it and just didn't think it was funny, which was why somebody coughed.

Upottery (n.)
That part of a kitchen cupboard which contains an unnecessarily large number of milk jugs.

Uttoxeter (n.)
A small but immensely complex mechanical device which is essentially the 'brain' of a modern coffee-vending machine, and which enables the machine to take its own decisions.

V

VALLETTA (n.)
An ornate head-dress or loose garment worn by a person in the belief that it renders them invisibly native and not like a tourist at all. People who don huge conical straw coolie hats with 'I Luv Lagos' on them in Nigeria, or fat solicitors from Tonbridge on holiday in Malaya who insist on appearing in the hotel lobby wearing a sarong know what we're on about.

VANCOUVER (n.)
The technical name for one of those huge trucks with whirling brushes on the bottom used to clean streets.

VENTNOR (n.)
One who, having been visited as a child by a mysterious gypsy lady, is gifted with the strange power of being able to operate the air-nozzles above aeroplane seats.

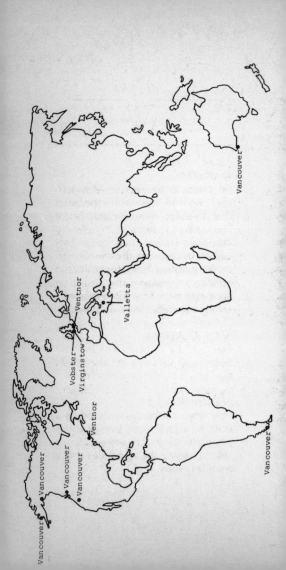

Virginstow (n.)
A Durex machine which doesn't have the phrase 'So was the Titanic' scrawled on it. The word has now fallen into disuse.

Vobster (n.)
A strain of perfectly healthy rodent which develops cancer the moment it enters a laboratory.

Weem

Whasset
Winksley
Wike
Wigan
Wetwang
Wroot
Worksop
Whissendine
Whaplode Drove
Wormelow Tump
Wendens Ambo
Writtle
Woolfardisworthy
Wembley
Wrabness
Wivenhoe
Warleggan
Woking
Widdicombe
Worgret
Wimbledon
West
Wittering

Wyoming
Willimantic
Winston-Salem

WARLEGGAN (n. archaic)
One who does not approve of araglins (q.v.).

WATH (n.)
The rage of Roy Jenkins.

WEEM (n.)
The tool with which a dentist can inflict the greatest pain. Formerly, which tool this was was dependent upon the imagination and skill of the individual dentist, though now, with technological advances, weems can be bought specially.

WEMBLEY (n.)
The hideous moment of confirmation that the diaster presaged in the ely (q.v.) has actually struck.

WENDENS AMBO (n.)

(Veterinary term.) The operation to trace an object swallowed by a cow through all its seven stomachs. Hence, also (1) an expedition to discover where the exits are in the Barbican Centre, and (2) a search through the complete works of Chaucer for all the rude bits.

WEST WITTERING (participial vb.)

The uncontrollable twitching which breaks out when you're trying to get away from the most boring person at a party.

WETWANG (n.)

A moist penis.

WHAPLODE DROVE (n.)

A homicidal golf stroke.

WHASSET (n.)

A business card in your wallet belonging to someone whom you have no recollection of meeting.

Whissendine (n.)
The noise which occurs (often by night) in a strange house, which is too short and too irregular for you ever to be able to find out what it is and where it comes from.

Widdicombe (n.)
The sort of person who impersonates trimphones.

Wigan (n.)
If, when talking to someone you know has only one leg, you're trying to treat them perfectly casually and normally, but find to your horror that your conversation is liberally studded with references to (a) Long John Silver, (b) Hopalong Cassidy, (c) the Hokey Cokey, (d) 'putting your foot in it', (e) 'the last leg of the UEFA competition', you are said to have committed a wigan.

The word is derived from the fact that sub-editors at ITN used to manage to mention the name of either the town Wigan, or Lord Wigg, in every fourth script that Reginald Bosanquet was given to read.

WIKE (vb.)
To rip a piece of sticky plaster off your skin as fast as possible in the hope that it will (a) show how brave you are, and (b) not hurt.

WILLIMANTIC (adj.)
Of a person whose heart is in the wrong place (i.e. between their legs).

WIMBLEDON (n.)
That last drop which, no matter how much you shake it, always goes down your trouser leg.

WINKLEY (n.)
A lost object which turns up immediately you've gone and bought a replacement for it.

WINSTON-SALEM (n.)
A person in a restaurant who suggests to their companions that they should split the cost of the meal equally, and then orders two packets of cigarettes on the bill.

WIVENHOE (n.)
The cry of alacrity with which a sprightly eighty-year-old breaks the ice on the lake when going for a swim on Christmas Eve.

WOKING (participial vb.)
Standing in the kitchen wondering what you came in here for.

WOOLFARDISWORTHY (n.)
A mumbled, mispronounced or misheard word in a song, speech or play. Derived from the well-known mumbled passage in *Hamlet*:

'. . . and the spurns,
That patient merit of the unworthy takes
When he himself might his quietus make
With a bare bodkin? Who woolfardisworthy
To grunt and sweat under a weary life?'

WORGRET (n.)
A kind of poltergeist which specialises in stealing new copies of the *A–Z* from your car.

Worksop (n.)
A person who never actually gets round to doing anything because he spends all his time writing out lists headed 'Things to Do (Urgent)'.

Wormelow Tump (n.)
Any seventeen-year-old who doesn't know about anything at all in the world other than bicycle gears.

Wrabness (n.)
The feeling after having tried to dry oneself with a damp towel.

Writtle (vb.)
Of a steel ball, to settle into a hole.

Wroot (n.)
A short little berk who thinks that by pulling on his pipe and gazing shrewdly at you he will give the impression that he is infinitely wise and 5 ft 11 in.

Wyoming (participial vb.)
Moving in hurried desperation from one cubicle to another in a public lavatory trying to find one which has a lock on the door, a seat on the bowl and no brown streaks on the seat.

YADDLETHORPE (vb.)
(Of offended pooves.) To exit huffily from a boutique.

YARMOUTH (vb.)
To shout at foreigners in the belief that the louder you speak, the better they'll understand you.

YATE (n.)
Dishearteningly white piece of bread which sits limply in a pop-up toaster during a protracted throcking (q.v.) session.

YEPPOON (n.)
One of the hat-hanging corks which Australians wear for making Qantas commercials.

YESNABY (n.)
A 'yes, maybe' which means 'no'.

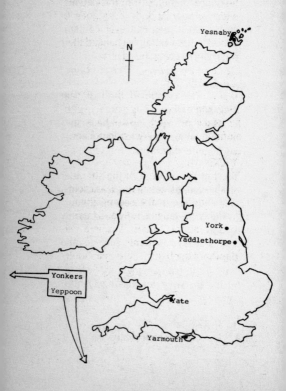

N

Yesnaby

York
Yaddlethorpe

Yonkers
Yeppoon

Yate

Yarmouth

YONDER BOGNIE (n.)
The kind of restaurant advertised as 'just three minutes from this cinema' which clearly nobody ever goes to and, even if they had ever contemplated it, have certainly changed their mind since seeing the advert.

YONKERS (n.)
(Rare.) The combined thrill of pain and shame when being caught in public plucking your nostril-hairs and stuffing them into your side-pocket.

YORK (vb.)
To shift the position of the shoulder straps on a heavy bag or rucksack in a vain attempt to make it seem lighter.
   Hence: to laugh falsely and heartily at an unfunny remark. 'Jasmine yorked politely, loathing him to the depths of her being' – Virginia Woolf.

Z

ZEAL MONACHORUM (n.)
(Skiing term.) To ski with 'zeal mona-chorum' is to descend the top three quarters of the mountain in a quivering blue funk, but on arriving at the gentle bit just in front of the res-taurant to whizz to a stop like a vic-torious slalom-champion.

Index of meanings

ballads, raucous old: *Banteer*
balls
   soggy, hairy: *Polperro*
   steel, rattling: *Writtle*
bamboo: *Blitterlees*
bands
   rock: *Throcking, Dittisham*
   rubber: *Monkstoft*
banks: *Albuquerque, Screggan,*
  Pentretafarnyfedw
Barbican Centre, the: *Wendens Ambo*
Barker, Ronnie: *Saffron Walden*
barmen
   aimless: *Todding*
   surly: *Goole*
barristers
   greasy: *Glazeley*
bars, wet: *Listowel*
bastards
   bloody rude: *Fovant*
   inconsiderate, stupid, filthy: *Dogdyke*
   in technical sense: *Gastard*
   lazy: *Abinger, Ozark*
   mad and/or lazy: *Boseman*
   six year old: *Little Urswick*
   smooth, beery: *Louth*
   smooth, lecherous, young: *Shirmers*
   smug, self-important, old: *Shenandoah*
   smug, shitty, Masonic: *Grimsby*
   vile, vain, rich: *Shalunt*
baths
   prunelike objects in: *Dewlish*
   round, rubbery objects in: *Dillytop*
bats
   hairy, harmless old: *Lossiemouth*
   incompetent, well-meaning old: *Jurby*
   stout, wooden: *Pelutho*
battleaxes, sharp, on castle wall: *Pabbay*
bddbbrrddrddrr, things that go: *Thrupp*

beating: *Aboyne*

bed

  areas to be avoided in: *Hobbs Cross*

  banana-shaped objects on: *Baumber*

  dreadful mistakes in: *Hagnaby*

  things found in: *Ballycumber*

  things that go wrong in: *Brecon*

  things that jump out of: *Duleek*

  unwelcome lumps in: *Tolob*

bedrooms, other people's: *Beaulieu Hill, Tibshelf*

behaviour, facetious, misguided: *Dockery*

behind

  dragging one leg: *Oundle*

  leaving one's hat: *Hidcote Bartram*

Belgians, hairy, religious: *Scethrog*

beliefs

  mistaken, humorous: *Dockery*

  mistaken, sartorial: *Twemlow Green*

berks

  unwanted: *Nubbock*

  short, pipe-smoking: *Wroot*

bicycle gears: *Wormelow Tump*

biros, leaky: *Pentretafarnyfedw*

birthdays, dwarfish: *Forsinain*

biscuits, digestive, religious: *Corstorphine*

biscuit tins: *Lindisfarne*

Blake's seven: *Clackavoid*

blobs

  bloody-minded: *Glossop*

  stubborn: *Quenby*

blowouts, oral: *Berkhamsted*

blue funk: *Zeal Monachorum*

blue murder: *Timble*

boards, don't forget: *Scremby*

bodkins, bare: *Woolfardisworthy*

book reviews: *Ripon*

books

  fat, expensive: *Great Tosson*

bubbles
   congealed, cheesy: *Eriboll*
   slurped, milky: *Pitlochry*
buffers
   boring old: *Ainderby Quernhow*
   insane sprightly old: *Wivenhoe*
   loathsome merry old: *Boothby Graffoe*
   pompous old: *Ainderby Steeple*
buggery: *Fairymount*
builders, murderous: *Hodnet*
bulbs, light: *Fring*
bulges
   cheesy: *Eriboll*
   huge, erotic: *Humby*
   huge, benign: *Botolphs*
   medium-sized, erotic: *Huby*
   persistent, unwanted: *Lower Peover*
   prestressed: *Bromsgrove*
   pustular: *Bilbster*
   tiny, erotic: *Budby*
   unwelcome, obvious: *Stebbing*
bumples, tiny: *Naples*
buns: *Brymbo*
bunches, usless: *Burton Coggles*
bunkers, nuclear: *Shenendoah*
burglars: *Taroom*
burns, non-poetic: *Hutlerburn*
buses
   desire on: *Abercrave*
   oversized: *Articlave*
   parts of: *Edgbaston*
   parts on: *Moffat*
bushes, small, humorous: *Grimmet*
buttons
   bacony: *Beccles*
   tummy: *Lowestoft*

cabers: *Camer*
cafes, nasty: *Cromarty*
camera shops: *Ainsworth*

candles, deformed: *Slubbery*
cans, tin: *Boscastle*
carcrushers, vital things that fall in: *Tyne and Wear*
carol singers, avoidance of: *Fulking*
carparks, automatic: *Nad*
carpet, rucked up edges of: *Thurnby*
cartoons
   sparing use of: *Great Tosson*
   vegetation in: *Grimmet*
cats, methods of dispatching: *Curry Mallet*
cavities
   definitely unhygenic: *Glutt Lodge, Henstridge*
   probably unhygenic: *Mankinholes*
chairs
   dismantled: *Blitterlees*
   plastic, sweaty: *Skibbereen*
   wickerwork: *Kettering*
chambermaids, grisly discoveries of: *Bedfont*
change
   small: *Boolteens*
   small, wet: *Goole*
Charles, Prince: *Ganges*
chef, loud wallies who call for the: *Haugham*
cheese, cottage: *Berkhamsted*
cheese-graters: *Abinger*
cheese, various sizes of: *Fraddam*
chess: *Bishop's Caundle*
chewing-gum: *Belper*
children
   small, inconvenient: *Glassel*
   small, rude, innocent: *Sneem*
   small, untidy: *Smearisary*
   small, untalented: *Papcastle*
   small, yelling: *Timble*
chimney, coming down the: *Deeping St Nicholas*
chocolates: *Bolsover, Cannock Chase*
Christmas, Father: *Deeping St Nicholas*

chuckles, chummy: *Lybster*
chumminess, man-to-man: *Tillicoultry*
cigarette ends, in lager: *Slumbay*
cigarettes
  two packets of: *Winston-Salem*
  untipped: *Scopwick*
cinema, just three minutes from this: *Yonder Bognie*
cleaning, dry: *Knaptoft*
cleaning ladies: *Spofforth*
cleavages, speleological, monstrous: *Simprim*
Cleese, John: *Goadby Marwood*
clifftops, silly little kids on: *Caarnduncan*
Clingfilm: *Amwlch*
clippers, gaff-rigged China: *Kanturk*
clocks
  alarm: *Duleek*
  cuckoo: *Penge*
clots, mad, patronising: *Largoward*
clubs, rubber: *Curry Mallet*
codgers
  boring, famous, old: *Boothby Graffoe*
  huge, wobbling, wheezing, old: *Kingston Bagpuise*
  stuffy, mediaeval, old: *Warleggan*
  twinkly, disgusting, old: *Feakle*
coffee-machines, intelligent: *Uttoxeter*
combs, clogged: *Haslebury Plucknett*
commissionaires
  boring: *Clabby*
  swinish: *Margate*
components
  small, meaningless: *Pimlico*
  vital, missing: *Exeter*
confetti, royal: *Didcot*
conversations
  interminable: *Ditherington*
  polite, interminable: *Clabby*
  polite, pointless: *Sittingbourne*
  shifting: *Glenties*

    wasted: *Harpenden*
corks, hat-hanging: *Yeppoon*
cosies, spare-toilet-roll: *Ossett*
cottages
    retirement: *Duncraggon*
    weekend: *Hull*
coughs
    gurgling: *Brisbane*
    throaty: *Dorchester*
cows: *Wendens Ambo*
craftwork: *Dalrymple*
cream, anti-wrinkle: *Melton Constable*
creeps
    mild: *East Wittering*
    gruesome: *Meathop*
crimes, ancient: *Burlingjobb*
crossings, pedestrian: *Boseman*
crotches, trouser: *Botley, Piddletrenthide*
crouches, upward: *Hucknall*
crying: *Babworth*
cubicles
    inaccessible: *Milwaukee*
    horribly soiled: *Wyoming*
cupboards
    jugs in: *Upottery*
    kites in: *Kanturk*
    saucepans in: *Cong*
    skeletons in: *Glemanuilt*
curses, Scottish: *Aird of Sleat*
cushions, by side of the road: *Edgbaston*
customs, charming pointless old: *Edgbaston*

Damocles, the Trewoofe of: *Trewoofe*
dances
    in street: *Droitwich, Stelling Minnis*
    of beerglasses: *Sketty*
darkness, groping for objects in: *Tegucigalpa*
dearies
    lovable mad old: *Bradworthy*
    soporific rabbity old: *Clabby*

decisions, wrong: *Huna*
decorations, Christmas: *Clovis, Chenies*
dentists: *Gipping, Gallipolli, Glutt Lodge*
dentists
  guerilla: *Beccles*
  violent: *Weem*
deposits, small, black, satisfying: *Tidpit*
desperation
  polite: *Iping*
  frankly rushed: *Wyoming*
determination, bloody-minded: *Oswestry*
devices
  agricultural: *Jarrow*
  humorous: *Barstibley*
dialogue, single page of: *Clackavoid*
diaries, meaningless entries in: *Epsom*
diarrhoea, verbal: *Ainderby Steeple*
dice: *Hoggeston*
dirt: *Sutton and Cheam*
disco, people who should have been left in the:
  Hagnaby
discrepancies, unaccountable: *Bodmin*
dishwashers: *Dobwalls*
disputes, poovy: *Agglethorpe, Yaddlethorpe*
dog-owners, cretinous: *Dogdyke*
dogs
  large, randy, teatime: *Scrabster*
  small, repulsive, snuffling: *Scorrier*
  small, moribund: *Scamblesby*
  small, viscious, yappy: *Baughurst*
dogturds, small but still nasty: *Bromsgrove*
doors
  deliberately obstructive: *Ramsgate*
  revolving, overpopulated: *Shifnal*
  things caused by walking into: *Sluggan*
doubleglazing, inhabitants of: *Harbottle*
downstairs lavatory, hats in: *Tweedsmuir*
drawbridges: *Araglin*
drawers, bottom: *Marlow, Pimlico*
dressing tables: *Boolteens*

dribble, infantile: *Halcro*
drink, philosophical state during: *Solent*
drinks, repellent: *Aasleagh, Naas*
drips, gooey, waxen: *Slubbery*
droplets
   hanging, stylish: *Berry Pomeroy*
   hanging, mobile: *Longniddry*
   persistent, trouser: *Wimbledon*
drunks
   uncomprehending: *Blithbury*
   unappealing: *Pleeley*
dry, not very: *Wrabness*
duffers, barking mad old: *Pant-Y-Wacco*
dwarves, nubile: *Forsinain*

ears
   outer: *Luffness*
   inner: *Nanhoron*
edicts, ancient: *Farduckmanton*
eggs, boiled: *Symond's Yat*
eighty year olds, bounding, refrigerated:
  Wivenhoe
elbows, sore: *Bures*
ends, long, thin, dangling: *Ranfurly*
engineers, telephone: *Lydiard Tregoze*
envelopes, dangerous: *Scramoge*
environments, dark, moist: *Huttoft*
epaulettes, useless: *Trossachs*
epiglottis, giant, waggling: *Ullingswick*
erasers, rubber: *Tampa*
escalators, cretins who block the: *Ullock*
euphemisms, senseless: *Fairymount*
evenings, wasted: *Lowther*
excrement, airborne: *Burlingjobb*
excuses
   feeble: *Dorridge*
   impromptu but still feeble: *Hastings*
   indignant: *Hoff*
   lame: *Ardscalpsie*
   ludicrous: *Brisbane*

folds, fleshy: *Lusby*
footballers, pansy: *Hoddlesden*
foreigners
    probably deaf or stupid: *Yarmouth*
    impersonation of: *Aberbeeg*
fowl-feeding: *Farduckmanton*
freemasonry: *Grimsby*
fridges
    congealed matter in: *Goosnargh*
    damp things in: *Nantwich*
    teeming with life: *Guernsey*
frowning, important: *Frolesworth*
fruit, theft of a single piece of: *Market Deeping*
furniture
    execrable: *Mapledurham*
    lavatorial, frilly: *Ossett*

Gable, Clark: *Epworth*
games
    ball: *Hoddlesden, Pelutho*
    board: *Bishop's Caundle, Hoggeston*
    indoor: *Aboyne*
    outdoor, East European: *Twomileborris*
gardening
    hopelessness of: *Crail*
    trousers of: *Broats*
gardens, embarrassing talks in: *Ambleside*
garments
    exotic, pretentious: *Shalunt*
    fatuous, foreign: *Valletta*
    gaberdine, ankle-length: *Flodigarry*
    peculiar, frightful: *Neen Sollars*
    woollen, knee-length: *Jurby*
gazes, shrewd, berkish: *Wroot*
gestures, ambiguous but bloody rude: *Fovant*
gin, price of: *Le Touquet*
girlfriend
    long forgotten except by wife: *Mavis Enderby*
girls, teenage in bedroom: *Tibshelf*
gizmos, plastic, metal, bakelite: *Pimlico*
glances, humorous, at blobs: *Swanage*

glass, pointless tapping on: *Stoke Poges*
globules, yellow, gummy, unpleasant: *Mugeary*
go, people who just won't: *Clunes*
goats
    jocular tedious old: *Barstibley*
    noisy tuneless old: *Royston*
golfing, overpaid twats who go: *Kitmurvy*
golfstrokes, homicidal: *Whaplode Drove*
goo, seagull: *Sutton and Cheam*
goodbyes, premature: *Hidcote Bartram*
gourmets, slithery: *Berry Pomeroy*
grass, intelligent forms of: *Trispen*
gravel, infuriating: *Crail*
Greer, Germaine: *Shrivenham*
grids, cattle: *Humber*
grocers, green: *Halifax, Smisby*
guards, railway: *Galashiels*
guilt, powerful: *Glemanuilt*
gumboots: *Burwash, Luffness*
gunge, green, shrubby: *Sadberge*
gurgling, involuntary, abdominal: *Tumby*
gusto, terrific, tuneless: *Royston*
gutters, dog's business clogging up the:
  Dogdyke

hair
    facial, bizarre: *Scethrog*
    greasy, legal: *Glazeley*
    pubic, in moussaka: *Scroggs*
    sprigs of, for chasing ants: *Monkstoft*
hairdressers, mad, Welsh: *Ardscalpsie*
handlebar moustaches, female: *Lossiemouth*
hands, clammy: *Meath*
hangovers, incapacitating: *Duntish*
hankies, worn knotted on head: *Sidcup*
hat behind, leaving ones: *Hidcote Bartram*
hatred, violent, by spouse: *Mavis Enderby*
hats
    furry, absurd: *Glinsk*
    gigantic, conical, coolie: *Valletta*
    large, ill-fitting collection of: *Tweedsmuir*

naff: *Sidcup*
heads, black: *Quabbs*
hedge, things to do behind one's front: *Todber*
herring fishermen: *Flodigarry*
history, lost in the mists of: *Hutlerburn*
holes
   bath overflow: *Polperro*
   nefarious use of: *Pode Hole*
   things which settle into: *Writtle*
   things which sit on *Dillytop*
horns
   large, uncomfortable: *Humby*
   long, ceremonial: *Hunsingore*
   moderate-sized but unconcealable: *Huby*
   small, Scandinavian: *Oswaldtwistle*
horror, inexpressible: *Maaruig*
horses, china, rude: *Barstibley*
hostesses, air: *Ewelme*
hotels
   incredibly dull: *Lamlash*
   mock-Tudor: *Melcombe Regis*
   shambolic, clanking: *Bonkle*
huffy exits: *Yaddlethorpe*
hutlers, clumsy: *Hutlerburn*
hunches, foolish, in the theatre: *Totteridge*
hymns: *Detchant, Royston*

ice, octogenarians under the: *Wivenhoe*
idea, not having the faintest: *Epsom, Osbaston*
identity cards, left at home: *Margate*
idiots
   roaring, pretentious: *Haugham*
   ludicrous, deluded: *Kibblesworth*
implements
   curious, horticultural: *Haxby*
   wooden, silly: *Ibstock*
   small, stout: *Naseby*
income tax, impossibility of doing: *Swanibost*
incontinence, reptilian: *Dunbar*
infants, small, naked, comical: *Barstibley*

inklings, tiny, stomach-curdling: *Ely*
interesting, than you, someone more: *Sconser*
interval, theatre bars in the: *Tabley Superior*
into each other, bumping: *Droitwich*
items
    nasal, airborne: *Scronkey*
    prunelike, waterlogged: *Dewlish*
    sticky, clammy: *Belper*
    sticky, furry: *Silloth*
    thin, circular, meaty: *Shanklin*
jackets
    dust: *Liff*
    hairy, stained: *Bradford*
    hideous, aquamarine: *Matching Green*
    hideous, casual: *Saffron Walden*
    hideous, emerald: *Sproston Green*
    loud check: *Louth*
    not quite long enough: *Stebbing*
Jenkins, Roy: *Wath*
jingles: *Dittisham*
jogging, suicide by means of: *Kingston
  Bagpuise*
Johnnies, rubber: *Sneem*
jokes, mild, for vicars: *Bude*
jokes, practical: *Araglin*
jokes, practical, spectacular: *Banteer*

keys, useless bunches of: *Burton Coggles*
kilts, hoary old gags about: *Glenwhilly*
kitchen walls: *Smearisary*
knees, sore: *Bures*
knobs
    medium-size: *Belper*
    pointless, stony: *Plympton*
knots, intricate: *Kanturk*

ladies, cleaning: *Clabby*
laughter, hearty, false: *York*
lawnmowers, frustrated: *Trispen*
leathery flapping bits: *Luppit*

legs
    things not underneath: *Limerigg*
    things underneath: *Hucknall*
    unwelcome things down: *Wimbledon*
    unwelcome things on: *Polloch*
    unwelcome things up: *Affpuddle*
    useless: *Clun*
    welcome things up: *Burwash*
    extremely unwelcome things up: *Scrabster*
Leith Police, the: *Tolstachaolais*
licking of envelopes: *Scramoge*
life, the British Way of: *Botcherby*
life, the facts of: *Ambleside*
lifts
    misuse of by weeds: *Nybster*
    silence in: *Emsworth*
lightbulbs, problems of disposing of: *Clathy*
limp bread: *Yate*
literary critics: *Ripon*
loaves, curious-shaped: *Bradworthy*
lobby, great oafs screeching in the: *Haugham*
looks
    lecherous: *Frosses*
    polite, angry: *Evercreech*
    superior, at shoes: *Dubuque*
    superior, in theatre: *Tabley Superior*
lounges, cocktail: *Melcombe Regis*
love, unrequited: *Lydiard Tregoze*
lovers, used up, by Germaine Greer:
  Shrivenham
luggage, ill-behaved: *Adlestrop*
lumps
    agricultural, aromatic: *Jarrow*
    cardboard, useful: *Ludlow*
    concrete, airborne: *Hodnet*
    disgusting, attached to face: *Kirby*
    dull, in suitcase: *Glassel*
    edible, steaming, irremovable: *Glossop*
    gristly, acrid: *Grimsby*
    gummy, shapeless: *Papcastle*

insular, inedible: *Hoylake*
powdery, floating: *Poges*
rural, underfoot: *Cairnpat*
small, awkward, dangerous: *Fraddam*
small, nasal: *Peebles*
tiny, in swimming trunks: *Lubcroy*
unwelcome, nocturnal, in front: *Humby*
unwelcome, nocturnal, underneath: *Tolob*
unwelcome, urban, all over: *Burlingjobb*
urban, overhead and underfoot: *Bromsgrove*

machines, contraceptive: *Virginstow*
mad, you don't have to be, etc.: *Snitterfield*
madmen, departed, in toasters: *Throckmorton*
making up: *Queenzieburn*
manholes, open, amusing: *Frimley*
manoeuvres, awkward, leaping: *Hobbs Cross*
maps, road: *Kalami*
margarine: *Darenth*
markets, super: *Duggleby, Flimby, Motspur,*
 Boscastle
mats, small, sopping: *Listowel*
matter, gaseous: *Eriboll*
mattresses
  banana-shaped: *Baumber*
  enormous, muscular: *Harbledown*
maybe, meaning no: *Yesnaby*
measures of distance
  (carparks): *Nad*
  (sheep): *Sheppey*
  (trousers): *Malibu*
  (tubes): *Frant*
measure of luminosity: *Blean*
measures of time
  (art galleries): *Frolesworth*
  (lifts): *Emsworth*
  (camera shops): *Ainsworth*
meat, ghastly surprises in: *Aigburth*
medallions, gold: *Herstmonceux*
men

175

    dismal, pedantic, little: *Benburb*
    pathetic, deluded, little: *Brough Sowerby*
    myopic, dangerous, little: *Low Eggborough*
merciless boiling: *Cong*
merry-go-rounds: *Adrigole*
mid-pee, pulling the chain in: *Tincleton*
milk-jugs, unnecessary numbers of: *Upottery*
mistakes
    Celtic, computer, spelling: *Maentwrog*
    embarrassing: *Tegucigalpa*
    horrifying, unavoidable: *Wigan*
mmm!!: *Hoylake*
moats: *Bealings*
modesty
    false: *Griminish*
    false, female: *Simprim*
moments
    awful: *Umberleigh*
    deeply embarrassing: *Lulworth*
    deeply unexciting: *Emsworth*
    utterly pant-wetting: *Wembley*
monasteries: *Corstorphine*
moods, irrational: *Cranleigh*
moors: *Luffness, Luffenham, Slogarie*
moron, not wanting to be thought a:
Frolesworth
morning
    five o'clock in the: *Bonkle*
    two o'clock in the: *Pott Shrigley*
    waking up in the: *Maaruig*
morsels, small, prominent, repulsive: *Kirby*
motorbikes
    feeling of new: *Nempnett Thrubwell*
    involuntary impersonation of: *Berepper*
moussaka, stout pubes in: *Scroggs*
movements
    bowel: *Glororum*
    fishlike: *Gipping*
    flabby: *Humber*
    futile, at post-offices: *Stoke Poges*

futile, at waiters: *Epping*
futile, in own house: *Kelling*
vague, manual, searching: *Scosthrop*
waggling, artistic: *Llanelli*
mumbling, as a career: *Woolfardisworthy*
Murmansk, things that shouldn't be in:
 Glentaggart
mush, dehydrated: *Pott Shrigley*

'n': *Nacton*
names, forgetting of: *Golant*
nastiness, hard-boiled: *Dobwalls*
neapolitan tubs, fist shoved into: *Blean*
news, astounding: *Jawcraig*
newspaper cuttings, comical: *Snitter*
newspapers, fascination of other peoples: *Corfe*
nipples, high-profile: *Budby*
nitwits, great steaming: *Duggleby*
no, expressed as yes: *Yesnaby*
nodules, rubber: *Pimperne*
nods, surly, from behind hedge: *Todber*
noises
    bubbling and inopportune: *Tumby*
    burbling and nocturnal: *Bonkle*
    discreet but unwelcome: *Affcot*
    distant and meaningless: *Amersham*
    humming and grinding: *Burleston*
    humming and groaning: *Milwaukee*
    grunting and considerate:
     Horton-cum-Studley
    grunting and satisfied: *Poona*
    gurgling and milky: *Pitlochry*
    gushing and cooing: *Oshkosh*
    loud and embarrassing: *Berepper*
    loud and clattering: *Clackmannan*
    loud and informative: *Taroom*
    loud and rattling: *Hoggeston*
    miniscule, worrying: *Fring*
    mumbling, uninterested: *Nazeing*
    painful and squeaky: *Skibereen*

quiet and rubbery: *Tampa*
screeching, Celtic: *Lochranza*
screeching, infantile: *Caarnduncan*
screeching, rural: *Mellon Udrigle*
squeaky, nylonish: *Screeb*
tatatting and satisfying: *Ibstock*
ticketatacketaticketting: *Seattle*
ticketatacktackatuckaticketting: *Trantlemore*
tiny and embarrassing: *Brompton*
tooting and puzzling: *Whissendine*
trumpeting, hippopotamoid: *Brompton*
whiffling, in lifts: *Burbage*
whirring and chuntering: *Ipswich*

noses
bleeding: *Burton Coggles*
erstwhile contents of: *Longniddry*
exterior features of: *Botolphs*
fascinating items in: *Massachussets*
noises made with: *Burbage*
things which come down from: *Des Moines*
tools for stuffing into: *Botusfleming*

nostalgic yearnings: *Aberystwyth*
nozzles, aircraft, strange powers over: *Ventnor*
number, wrong, so she claims: *Kurdistan*

nurds
lanky, Scandinavian: *Ullock*
incredible little: *Corfu*
piddling, in your lavatory: *Tincleton*
preeping: *Widdicombe*
tittering, white-collar: *Snitterby*

objects
fantastically dull: *Lamlash*
banana-shaped: *Baumber*
bloody-minded: *Ardslingnish*
clammy, inedible: *Amwlch*
deformed: *Duddo*
elephantine: *Clackmannan*
flimsy, intriguing: *Corfu*
frilly: *Ossett*

grisly: *Cairnpat*
heavy, with toes on: *Clun*
horrible, roomy: *Mapledurham*
long-handled: *Botusfleming*
lost, found again: *Winkley*
massive, wooden, airborne: *Camer*
plastic, pretentious: *Brumby*
small, priceless, in pieces: *Tyne and Wear*
small, boring: *Nazeing*
sticky, permanent: *Dipple*
sticky, wooden: *Cotterstock*
strange, culinary: *Cong*
tiny, disgusting: *Chipping Ongar*
tiny, pointless: *Didcot*
unappealing, lonely: *Brymbo*
wet, cold, enormous: *Trewoofe*
with bumps on: *Bolsover*
with holes in, artistic: *Bromsgrove, Dalrymple*
officers, retired, army, raving: *Pant-y-Wacco*
offices, inhabitants of: *Clovis, Brough Sowerby,
Snitterby*
office walls, comical cuttings on: *Snitter*
oiks, loudmouthed, tedious: *Goadby Marwood*
Olsson, Nigel: *Throcking*
ooze, yellow: *Clonmult*
orchestra pits, spittle in: *Ullapool*
orchestras, people who conduct from audience:
Thrumster
orgasm, multiple: *Papworth Everard*
ornaments, misapplied: *Bishop's Caundle*
overalls, inky: *Hibbing*

pain and shame: *Yonkers*
pains
 sudden: *Acle*
 tools for inflicting: *Weem*
paintbrushes, cheap: *Aith*
paint smudges, expensive: *Dalrymple*
paintstirrers: *Cotterstock*
pyjamas, muslim: *Albuquerque*

pangs, terrible: *Lydiard Tregoze*
panic
   in airport: *Hever*
   in corridor: *Ditherington*
   in lavatory: *Great Wakering*
panther sweat, erotic properties of: *Dunbar*
parked cars, hooting at: *Tooting Bec*
particles, nasal: *Massachussetts*
parties
   anger after: *Heanton Punchardon*
   crud under sofa after: *Silloth*
   dreadful guests at: *Nubbock, Oughterby*
   drink running out at: *Aasleagh*
   erks you can't get away from at: *East Wittering*
   teenage, steamy: *Frosses*
parts, of speech, crucial, obscured: *Dorchester*
parts, private, had by dog for lunch: *Scorrier*
patches, wet, underarm: *Pitsligo*
patches, wet, underbottom: *Hobbs Cross*
paving stones: *Affpuddle*
pebbles, wet, shiny: *Glassel*
pedants: *Ainderby Quernhow*
pee, inability to with audience present:
   Kettleness
peer groups: *Caarnduncan*
pellets, unmentionable: *Peebles*
pencil sharpenings, giant: *Blitterlees*
penises, moist: *Wetwang*
pens, lack of: *Aynho*
people
   cringing, irritating: *Greeley*
   frantic, disorganised: *Worksop*
   large groups of miserly: *Bodmin*
   large groups of helpful grunting:
     Horton-Cum-Studley
   medium sized clumps of enraged: *Dolgellau*
   niggling: *Scranton*
   small families of horrible: *Molesby*
   small groups of whiffling: *Burbage*

   smooth, greedy: *Winston-Salem*
   underprivileged, leg-wise: *Wigan*
   unshaven, maddening: *Draffan*
   vast, wobble-cheeked: *Humber*
   who give themselves the biggest slice: *Finuge*
perpetuity, in: *Cotterstock*
photographs, passport: *Banff*
picnic spots
   mildly uncomfortable: *Munderfield*
   splattered with gore: *Meathop*
pigs, matching: *Tibshelf*
piles, unstable: *Boscastle*
pillows: *Abilene*
pimples, volcanic: *Bilbster*
pins
   danger: *Acle*
   safety: *Lubcroy*
pipers: *Lochranza*
places, safe: *Fiunary*
plaster, torn off skin: *Wike*
pleasure, idiosyncratic, revolting: *Glororum*
plucking of nostril hairs: *Yonkers*
plugs, bath: *Dillytop, Twomileborris*
plumbing noises: *Bonkle*
pockets
   omnivorous: *Nantucket*
   upholstered: *Hassop*
points, sound made by trains crossing:
   Trantlemore
poles, strong desire to grasp: *Abercrave*
policemen, skin of: *Melton Constable*
politicians
   rabid, left-wing, rich: *Quedgeley*
   ridiculous, furry-hatted: *Glinsk*
polo: *Ganges*
poltergeists, resident in car: *Worgret*
poodles, glass: *Tibshelf*
pools, warm, edible: *Hoylake*
pooves: *Yaddlethorpe, Agglethorpe*
pornography, the making of: *Papworth Everard*

181

positions, switches which seem to be off in both: *Ockle*
potatoes
   fear of: *Peoria*
   misshapen: *Duddo*
pouches, small, humorous: *Glenwhilly*
poultry-keepers: *Goosecruives*
prats, overdressed, incompetent: *Kitmurvy*
prefaces: *Querrin*
pretences
   absurd: *Dogdyke*
   seasonal: *Fulking*
prongs
   bent: *Bromsgrove*
   concealed: *Hadzor*
   clogged with sludge: *Henstridge*
   truncated: *Baldock*
prunelike extremities: *Dewlish*
pubs
   berks in: *Louth, Boothby Graffoe*
   waiting for the, to open: *Luffenham*
puddings, miserable: *Nutbourne*
puddles
   exterior: *Burwash, Affpuddle*
   interior: *Goole, Sketty*
punishment, capital, in schools: *Little Urswick*
purpose, unfathomable: *Haxby*
pus, scarlet: *Buldoo*
push taps, embarrassments caused by: *Botley*
pyramids, metallic: *Boscastle*

queues; *Duggleby, Evercreech, Foindle Twomileborris*

railway food: *Amwlch*
races, three-legged: *Shifnal*
raincoats, expensive: *Trossach*
rashes, leg: *Ganges*
rattling, senseless: *Amersham*
reactions, chemical, unedifying: *Bradford*

Rees, Nigel
   lower half: *Twemlow Green*
   upper half: *Sproston Green*
   horrible ensemble: *Matching Green (ironic)*
relish trays: *Clonmult, Sadberge, Buldoo*
remarks
   own, rather amusing, unheard: *Dorchester,*
    Umberleigh
   pompous, hypocritical, clichéd: *Reculver*
removals, non-furniture: *Dipple*
requests, whining, unwelcome: *Quall*
restaurants, unfussy, unusual menu: *Curry*
  Mallet
revelations, personal with stomach-rumble:
  Tumby
Richard the Third: *Oundle*
ripping, of skin: *Wike*
rights
   ancient, pebbly: *Pevensey*
   ancient, with midgets: *Forsinain*
roads, signposting of: *Botcherby*
rock
   quiet and persistent: *Crail*
   loud and boring: *Throcking*
   loud and persistent: *Dittisham*
rubbish, vital, in dustcart: *Nottage*
rucksacks: *York*
rugs, horse-shoe-shaped, fluffy: *Luton*
rulers, noises made by: *Thrupp*
runs, token: *Sturry*
Ryvita, consistency of: *Naples*

sachets, impenetrable: *Naugatuck*
sacking: *Tillicoultry*
safe places: *Fiunary*
salami: *Shanklin*
sandwiches
   bacon: *Beccles*
   in London: *Darenth*
   on trains: *Amwlch*

sheets, bloody awful nylon: *Brecon*
shifting, anxious: *Iping*
shingle, collectors of: *Pevensey*
shirts
   beer down: *Tulsa*
   open to waist: *Herstmonceux*
   stabbing: *Acle*
shoes, wrong sort of: *Dubuque*
shops, dress: *Dolgellau*
shops
   maddening, camera: *Ainsworth*
   shoe, idiot: *Kibblesworth*
   with stupid names: *Drebley*
shouting at foreigners: *Yarmouth*
showers, agonising: *Alltami*
sick, off wrong side of boat: *Silesia*
side
   things on the other: *Quenby*
   things that stick out the: *Aith*
   things written on the: *Dorridge*
sideburns, extensive, scrofulous: *Galashiels*
signposts, pathetic attempt at proper:
  Botcherby
silences, ghastly: *Lulworth*
silver paper against teeth: *Tingrith*
singers, carol, hiding from: *Fulking*
sixteen
   stone men on last legs: *Kingston Bagpuise*
   year olds on heat: *Frosses*
six times before, stories heard: *Smarden*
skiing: *Zeal Monachorum*
skin
   flaps of: *Scopwick*
   twists of: *Kerry*
sleep
   muck in eyes after: *Mugeary*
   things which stop you getting to: *Bursledon*
   things which shouldn't have gone to: *Clun*
slimming, feeble dishonest shot at:
  Berkhamsted

sludge, brittle: *Cromarty*
smells, horrible: *Keele*
smiles
  frozen, horrified: *Sneem*
  grim, determined: *Smarden*
  shiny, meaningless: *Ewelme*
smoking, excuses for: *Brisbane*
smutty postcards: *Snitterfield*
snacks, nasty: *Nantwich*
sneezing
  failure to: *Amersham*
  horribly violent success at: *Sconkey*
snippets, hairy: *Hathersage*
snow, wedges of lurking: *Trewoofe*
socks, contents of: *Skenfrith*
sofa, things spotted from: *Chenies*
solicitors, fat, from Tonbridge: *Valletta*
something or other, profound feelings of:
  Hambledon
sopping, shopping: *Sotterley*
soup
  exotic, made from moats: *Bealings*
  packet: *Poges*
  splattered: *Papple*
  tomato: *Scranton*
space and timelessness: *Hambledon*
spasms, massive facial: *Jawcraig*
spit: *Gallipolli*
spoonful, eggy: *Symonds Yat*
sprigs, dangling, colourful: *Chenies*
squeezing
  cosmetic: *Quabbs*
  religious: *Clenchwarton*
squiggles, financial: *Albuquerque*
stains
  inky: *Hibbing*
  Marmite: *Sutton and Cheam*
  trousers, own fault: *Piddletrenthide*
  trousers, not own fault: *Botley*
staircases, winding: *Harbledown*

tips, felt: *Scremby*
Titanic, so was the: *Virginstow*
toast: *Burnt Yates*
toasters: *Throckmorton, Yates*
toenails, contents of: *Tidpit*
toes, slime on: *Deal*
tools, painful, oral: *Weem*
tongs, silver, for poking Freemasons: *Grimsby*
torches, dim: *Blean*
towels, damp: *Wrabness*
tractors, dung-spreading: *Jarrow*
trains
   impersonation of: *Trantlemore, Seattle*
   royal: *Didcot*
   departed without one: *Dunboyne*
   tickets: *Nantucket*
tramps, mad, jabbering: *Theakstone*
trimphones, impersonation of: *Widdecombe*
tripping over carpet: *Thurnby*
trolleys, rogue: *Motspur*
trousers
   elderly: *Broats*
   fissile: *Nether Poppleton*
   garish: *Twemlow Green*
   inflatable: *Huby*
   roguish: *Minchinhampton*
   soaking: *Esher*
   stained: *Botley, Piddletrenthide*
   too long: *Malibu*
   wooden: *Goosecruives*
   wrong pair of: *Duggleby*
trouts, fierce old: *Baughurst*
trucks, street-cleaning: *Vancouver*
trunks, swimming: *Lubcroy*
truth, palpable: *Hoff*
tubes
   in London: *Amersham, Chicago, Frant*
   in meat: *Aigburth*
   in spring: *Pitsligo*
tubs, impenetrable: *Polloch*

turn-ups, fertile: *Huttoft*
twats, annoying: *Thrumster*
twitching, uncontrollable: *West Wittering*
twerps, bicycle-oriented: *Wormelow Tump*

umbrella stands: *Clackmannan*
underblankets, lumpy: *Tolob*
underclothes, bestrewn: *Adlestrop*
underpant, half an: *Scrabby*
undressing, watching other people: *Beaulieu Hill*
urges, violent: *Kent*
urinals, humiliation at: *Percyhorner*
usherettes: *Blean*

vampire attacks: *Spittal of Glenshee*
veneer, chipboard: *Mapledurham*
vicars, entertainment of: *Bude*
virgins, absence of at weddings: *Shirmers*

wads, misshapen, squashy: *Pudsey*
waggling, theatrical: *Llanelli*
waiters
   blind: *Epping*
   dozy: *Aynho*
wally, a: *Clovis*
walks, funny: *Goadby Marwood*
wallets: *Whasset*
walls
   with worrying holes in: *Pode Hole*
   satisfying: *Skellow*
   daubed: *Smearisary*
wartlike objects: *Kirby Misperton*
washing up
   failure to finish properly: *Abinger*
   nasty bits in the: *Scullet, Hadzor*
waves
   token: *Sturry*
   unnecessary: *Largoward*
   up trouser: *Malibu*